A Midsummer Night in Oz

Book 6 of the Mari Fable Mysteries

Emily Fluke

Also by Emily Fluke

-The Mari Fable Mysteries

Death of a Fairy Tale

Kidnapping the Classics

The Pinocchio Project

A Grimm Haunting

Snow Spell's Heartbreak

A Midsummer Night in Oz

-The Bewitcher's Beach Paranormal Cozy Mystery Series

Be Careful What You Witch For

Magic, Movies, and Murder

Squeaks and Spooks

Summoning, Skating, and Skulls

Book 3 (releasing 2024)

-The Garden Party Ghostess

Be sure to snag the prequels to both the Mari Fable Mysteries, and the Bewitcher's Beach Paranormal Cozy Mysteries FREE from my newsletter: The Glass Coffin and Be Careful What You Witch For.

https://landing.mailerlite.com/webforms/landing/y4h6c8

"To Mari Fable fans, you gave Mari, Kai, Wendy, and Scarlet a life beyond the pages. Thank you."

Prologue

Dear Journal,

The crying never stops. From me, from my baby, and from my best friend. Abundant tears that could drown the entire city of San Francisco flow from us all.

Four months ago I gave birth to Jack Frost, my work 'partner' Detective Wilhelm murdered the Snow Queen, and then my husband and I accidentally got Sherlock Holmes killed. See why I cry a lot? Actually, I cry because I'm exhausted since my magical snow child screams when he should be sleeping. He wants to use his dangerous ice magic, mommy says no—cue the crying. From both of us. Oh, and about my bff, Scarlet, she cries because she is an emotional pregnant lady with Rapunzel in her womb. It's intense. On top of that, her fiancé is struggling with PTSD from his time as Pinocchio. He mostly goes by 'Carlos' now in order to separate himself from the author Carlo Collodi.

As for the rift between our world and the alternate universe we call Storyland, it's still there. It's still in the center of Pioneer Park, partially protected by Red Riding Hood's magical hood—Watson was not. The Brothers Grimm promised Sherlock's partner would help me solve the mystery of the rift but he abandoned his post when more of

1

Storyland spilled over into San Francisco. The truth is, I peeled the hood back a bit too far when Detective Wilhelm threatened to shoot me in the face (I was scared, okay?), and now the hood is no longer only mine.

The magic responds to Scarlet again too. She could take it and become The Keeper of Stories again. Together, we've agreed to leave it alone because it is the only protection between our home and the war that rages in Storyland. It hangs by a thread and the story world's influence over San Francisco grows worse, but I refuse to see what'll happen to my city if we take the hood away completely.

So, the Brothers Grimm gods have recruited me to save the world —actually, both worlds.

If only I had their magic... and a full night's sleep I might have half a chance. Send an IV of caffeine and anything with cheese, because I need energy STAT.

Chapter One

(4 months later)

The strength of a determined baby's grip was unmatched even by an immortal slayer of wolves and witches. Technically, I had yet to kill the witch, and I was no longer an eternal being protected by the hood granted to The Keeper of Stories. But as an exhausted mom pulling an all-nighter in a Facebook Marketplace rocking chair with a fussy baby, I was just as much of a baddie. Not that anyone asked.

I wrestled the shard of ice from Jack's pudgy fingers before the sharp edge could slice through the rolls of baby fat between his knuckles. A feral guttural scream erupted from the bowels of his chunky baby belly. Clearly, he disagreed with me taking away the product of his own *Jack Frost* magic.

"Shhh," I begged, eyes darting to Wendy's closed door. The poor girl needed her sleep before her school's Peter Pan play debuted and she took the stage acting as the main character. I held my breath and waited to see if the exploding shriek woke anyone in our little condominium. Thankfully, not a creature was stirring, not even my husband. I blew out a breath and sunk deeper into the worn chair.

Alone I sat, rocking and rocking and rocking until Jack finally gave up using his winter magic and his eyelids grew heavy. Despite the weight of my own eyelids and the bags that piled like wet sand beneath my eyes, my mind buzzed with the words of Jacob and Wilhelm Grimm.

The world is ending and because you killed the man trying to stop it, the responsibility to save us all is now yours.

As if reacting to my disturbing thoughts, Jack twitched and burbled angrily. His fingers went from pink and warm to icy blue in an instant.

"If only I hadn't killed Sherlock Holmes," I mumbled. The low vibration of my voice soothed him as he snuggled his doughy cheek into the fabric of the robe. "If only I weren't The Keeper of Stories," I said, testing to see if Jack slept better when I spoke. He passed the test with flying colors when a soft snore rose and fell and his four-month-old body went limp in my arms. "Maybe it's time to answer the call of the gods."

A frown twisted my face as my gaze fell to the papers stacked haphazardly on the coffee table. After the gods' unwelcome visit to the hospital four months earlier, they'd graced me with their obnoxious presence a dozen more times. In fact, they hardly left me alone, until all at once they vanished, unreachable, never-returning and I was remiss to admit that I'd rather deal with their brotherly banter than wonder where they'd gone.

Time and time again they had haunted me during a precious moment of sleep between Jack's crying, or when I'd arrived at Wendy's school for afternoon pickup, or that time I tried to order a coffee at the corner Starbucks and suddenly *whoosh*, two ghosts appeared in front of me and I threw my scalding hot cup of much-needed latte at the poor barista who'd wrongly assumed I was dissatisfied with my service.

Oh, how I longed for a taste of a latte right now. Or a slice of cheesecake. Or anything to distract me from the pile of papers. The leaning tower of printed articles and Post-It notes were months' worth of studying and research of *Little Red Riding Hood*. I didn't know the details of why the gods believed this fairy tale was the origin of all our troubles, other than the existence of the hood itself, but I didn't question it. I merely studied. And studied. And studied some more.

During long nights just like this one, I balanced Jack in the crook of my arm while blinking sleep from my eyes. He'd refused to relax unless I held him and I'd refused to stop studying, hoping that I could make sense of the story. If I understood *Little Red Riding Hood*, maybe I'd understand how to fix the rift. How had the hood come into existence in the first place? Unfortunately, the original Keeper of Stories couldn't remember the details.

Scarlet knew she was like Red—a girl in a similar retelling called *The Little Cloak Girl*. She knew she'd wandered the woods just as Red did. She didn't know when she'd become The Keeper of Stories, how long she'd been lost in the woods, or when her hood had become imbued with magic, granting her immortality and driving her to correct fairy tales across time and space.

"Time and space," I muttered in a mocking tone, attempting to sound like Jacob Grimm. "Such things simple humans do not fully comprehend." I thrust a finger into the air as if I was Wilhelm Grimm arguing with his brother. "You were a human once too, Jake. Don't forget humans and unreliable narrators are one and the same." After switching back to Jacob's tinny voice, I finished the memory. "Narrators are gods, Will. Eternal, reincarnating, all-powerful, *gods*." Apparently, Wilhelm couldn't argue with that because their conversation had ended, and they'd blinked at me. I'd retorted with a snide comment of my own. *I'm surprised you're giving all this metaphorical power to the narrators.*

That was when they'd vanished, disappearing in a fade of speechlessness and I'd never seen or heard from them again. Except for a thought, a single thought that overcame me in a mix of their voices and mine.

Narrators, authors, and gods are all creators, one and the same.

How could a narrator be both a human and a god? The Grimm brothers made about as much sense as Jack's baby babble.

I shook off the memory, leaned forward with a grunt, and plucked a printed article from the top of the stack. My gaze trailed the lines, reading each word but remembering none of it. Trapped in a catatonic state of exhaustion and an unquiet mind, I blew out a breath and dropped my hand. The paper fell from my fingers, drifting to the floor like a brittle leaf in the dead of fall.

After a moment of musing over whether to put Jack in his crib or stay here for the night, I reached for the TV remote with my bare toes. With the most exercise I'd managed all month, I pinched the remote between both feet and brought it close enough to reach. I flicked on the TV and selected an episode of *Buffy the Vampire Slayer* I'd seen a hundred times.

The familiar characters soothed me but did nothing to distract my mind. My mind wandered to the history of *Little Red Riding Hood*, the only story to appear across dozens of cultures, times, and places. Each story was almost the same with a young girl or woman eaten. Some-times the villain was a spirit, a demon, an ogre, or a wolf. Despite the differences, the stories shared a similar message: *the world is a dangerous place, be careful and don't go alone.* But it wasn't the theme, the moral, or even the demon that clung to the recesses of my mind and refused to let me sleep. It was the narrator. Each version was written with a voice I recognized. A voice that spanned to other fairy tales I'd had to study since becoming The Keeper of Stories.

Another voice jarred my thoughts. Buffy shouted at Angel on the TV screen and I squinted at the TV, annoyed that it failed to relax my brain's buzzing. For once, Jack wasn't screaming his head off which meant I needed to take this precious moment and squeeze in some shut-eye. Once I relaxed.

Since the episode didn't work, I leaned my butt to the side and dug out my phone from between the cushion and the chair's arm. Scrolling social media only left my heart sinking further and further. Every other post was a prayer request for another disaster in the city or a call for donations to an overflowing clinic. The headline of a news video caught my eye. *Woman Claims Identity As Fairy Queen At Serial Killer Sighting.* I tapped the button to play the video. It showed a beautiful woman grabbing the microphone from the newscaster who asked her to comment on the burning building behind her. "I am Titania!" she shouted, ignoring his question. "Queen of the Fairies."

"Oh crap," I breathed. People almost never knew they'd become a magical character from a fairy tale or a story from classic literature. The story aura was getting worse, bolder, more obvious, and I knew why. I'd partially stripped Red's hood from where its magic had sewn into the rift and produced a temporary seal between Storyland and the human world.

The newscaster nodded and tried to redirect the woman back to the situation at hand. "Titania, is it? Are you a resident here at Oasis Apartment Complex?"

Before the woman could answer, two nearly identical men, both short, red-faced, and significantly overweight scurried from around the burning building and interrupted her interview. "He's here!" One of them burped. "The man who set our home on fire. The man who killed and ate our brother—"

I shut the screen off before the video could traumatize me any more than it already had. My heart slammed against my ribcage as if I'd just run a marathon, and the phone almost slipped from my sweaty hand.

"Are you okay?"

I startled at the voice, jarring Jack from his snuggled spot against my chest. My husband rubbed his eyes and crossed from the bedroom through the kitchen and into the living room as the baby whined and fussed. Jack threw his head side to side and his face was pinched in distraught anger.

"I'm not okay," I said. Tears welled in my eyes as Jack burst into another grating cry and ice chilled his body from the inside out.

Kai ran his fingers through his hair and stooped over me, scooping our son into his arms. "Go to bed," he said over the waning cries.

I shook my head. "It doesn't matter. I won't sleep. It's getting worse, Kai." Concern wrinkled his forehead where his overgrown waves of messy hair hung. "I've been ignoring it for too long. The headlines are fairy tale problems. I just saw a video of a woman calling herself a character from *A Midsummer Night's Dream* and the fat men looked just like pigs—" my throat squeezed until my voice no longer worked. I cleared it and kept going while my husband bounced Jack and stared at me, his eyes full of love and fear. "The pig men. You know? With the cannibal?"

"The pig men and the cannibal? I don't remember that fairy tale," he said.

"I'm serious!" I threw my hands up in a surrender of frustration. Nothing could stop the sob from overflowing into a fountain of tears and ugly crying now.

"I know, I—wait, *The Three Little Pigs*?" he asked.

I nodded, unable to speak through the wracking sobs. "One of them is dead, and it's my fault. I've done nothing for four months. I can't make sense of Red or the rift or anything! And where the hell are the Grimms?" I spoke through gritted teeth as tears streamed down my cheeks and soaked the milk stains on my robe.

"We've tried," he said. "You have tried, Mari. But you can't solve an impossible puzzle. Without the hood, you can't find the people that the story aura has chosen to become characters. But if you take the hood, the rift becomes an open gate between Storyland and our world, and then how many more pig men and cannibals will run around San Francisco's streets?"

To the people in the condo next door, our conversation may have sounded rough, like my husband wasn't considering my desperate cries. Not to mention insane. But Kai knew exactly what I needed—the truth. I was stuck between a rock and a hood with no hints or clues other than what the gods of the story world had left me with. *We believe the answer to separating the entangled worlds is in the origin of its blending when Red lost her way.*

Red Riding's hood was hanging by a literal thread as it patched the hole between the human world and the world of fairy tale characters. The magical fabric that had given me immortality and had led me to innocent people plagued with the story aura, was a Band-Aid on a tear in the fabric of reality. It stopped villains and dangerous magic from spilling over into San Francisco, but it also meant I couldn't resume my role as The Keeper of Stories. And when the story aura seeped through, I was powerless to stop the disaster that ensued—AKA pig men and cannibals.

I swallowed another rising sob and met my husband's eyes across the room. He took a seat on the couch kitty-corner to the rocking chair and offered me a sad smile. All I wanted to do was curl up in his arms and fall asleep in the comfort of his hold. While I fantasized about cuddling with him, a thought struck me.

"The puzzle isn't unsolvable," I said with a nervous sigh. "Almost every Red Riding Hood story ends the same. She gets eaten."

"What are you saying?" He spoke quietly so he wouldn't disturb the snoring child in the crook of his arm. Based on the crinkle between his eyebrows and the twist of his lips, he knew exactly what I was saying. "You can't."

"The fairy tales in Storyland replay over and over and the characters reincarnate. The wolf is there, but he has no Red to eat. All the stories' endings that I've thwarted likely have the same problem, and it boils down to the first one. At least that's what the Grimms said, so I have to—"

"No." Kai shook his head, knocking his shaggy hair about. "No way. You're not going there to sacrifice yourself. I can't let you do that."

"Not even if it makes the world a safer place for our children?" I asked.

The pain in his eyes was palpable. Now all I wanted was to take him into *my* arms. To run my fingers through his hair and the soft spot of my thumb over the scruff on his jaw. I wanted to comfort him as easily as he'd soothed our son.

I wanted a world safe for both of them, and for Wendy. But I also refused to leave them behind, motherless, wifeless, heartbroken.

Another rock. Another hard place.

"What if there's another way?" I whispered. A glimmer of hope flickered in Kai's eyes. Or maybe it was just the reflection of Buffy flashing across the screen. "What if I can continue Sherlock's work and seal the rift from the other side?"

"And leave you trapped there?"

I shook my head. "I'm not a character, and since I don't belong, I have this feeling…" The narrator of each of the stories popped into my head. In some fairy tales this powerful being was referenced as a real person. I couldn't quite make sense of it, but who could after only two hours of sleep? Finally, I stood and shuffled past the coffee table to bend over and plant a kiss on his temple. "I'm going to go to bed."

"That's it? You decided you'll seal yourself into an alternate reality and then you just say *goodnight and good luck*?" Kai's colloquial way of speaking nudged a smile onto my face that I didn't think I'd had the energy to hold.

I shrugged. "It's better than being eaten."

Chapter Two

"How now, spirit! Whither wander you?"

— William Shakespeare, A Midsummer Night's
Dream

A relentless ring split through my head. I rolled over in the fluff of a tangled comforter and slapped my hand against the nightstand. Had I set an alarm to nurse newborn Jack? Was Detective Wilhelm calling to alert me of a dead body, murdered on top of my *If you're not delivering cheesecake, go away!* doormat? No, the detective was the dead one and Jack was no longer a newborn but a baby of four-months old. I snagged the phone and squinted at the painfully bright screen.

The image of a woman with immaculate red curls covered the screen. The picture showed both Scarlet and Wendy taking a side-by-side selfie with scrunched noses and their tongues sticking out. Sleepy confusion dragged my mind through the memory of that day when we'd gone ice skating at the seasonal rink in the center of San Francisco. Jack had happily soaked in the icy air while Kai insisted on immersion therapy by facing his fear of winter head on. Carlos got down on one knee, proposing to his beloved girlfriend and Scarlet screamed.

I screamed too, but when Wendy screamed, it was for a different reason. The earthquake had struck, knocking my daughter to her knees against the hard ice. Scarlet had spilled her hot cocoa down the front of her cream peacoat, destroying the opportunity for engagement photos, and Kai was traumatized all over again.

The phone's screen went black, swiping the recent memory away in an instant. I blinked as my brain caught up with the here and now. I was alone in bed, Kai likely fell asleep on the couch with Jack in his arms, and it was only a couple of hours until my morning alarm would blare. Like a zombie, I'd drag myself from bed and help Wendy prepare for her big performance.

An obnoxious ring startled a gasp from me, and the phone brightened again. I swiped to answer Scarlet's call since I was fully lucid now.

"I'm in labor," she said, her voice cracking with fear. "Get your butt here right—"

"Coming," I said as I threw my legs over the side of the bed. Without even changing, I charged for the door. Kai gave me a lazy smile as his eyes slid open. Buffy was paused mid-fight on the TV and a message appeared on the screen. *Continue watching?* "Scarlet is having the baby, I have to go. She refuses to go to the hospital and Carlos will probably pass out."

"Hey!" he said groggily, then covered Jack's ears and dropped his voice to a whisper. "Not every guy faints at the sight of childbirth."

I laughed as I crossed the length of the living room. "You did."

He shrugged. "You've got me there. Call me when you get to her and take your time. I've got Wendy's costume."

I thanked him and shoved my fist through the sleeve of a rain jacket. After slipping my feet into a pair of sneakers with the heels tamped down and laces still tied, I ducked out the door. San Francisco's weather had been unpredictable since the snowstorm caused by the Snow Queen's tale. We'd even had a very unusual tornado watch, and I suspected Dorothy and her little dog Toto might appear in the park any day now.

The short walk to Carlos and Scarlet's apartment revived me. Cool air blasted my face and scattered rain fell in fits and starts, dotting the stained city pavement with what looked like tears from a world in mourning. The Grimm gods seemed to believe it would only get worse and worse with time, but I'd found no solution in the suggestions they'd given me.

I darted across an intersection just before the crosswalk time ran out and shoved my hands into the jacket's pockets. Skyscrapers lined the city sidewalk, towering over me as they stretched into the low-hanging clouds. A gust of wind ruffled the hood of my rain jacket and, for once, I longed for Red's hood. The invisible force of immortality and protection. The magic that had guided me to the people who'd been unlucky enough for the story aura to choose. Of course, if those people already had the personality of a certain character, they were bound to be selected—which, in my opinion, made the villains all that much more creepy.

I shivered at the thought of whoever the Big Bad Wolf from *The Three Little Pigs* had been even before the story aura found him. *Ick.*

After climbing the stairs, I wiped the wetness of my soles on Carlos and Scarlet's doormat—a rough rug with cheesy emojis—and used my key to enter.

Inside, humid warmth surrounded me. Scarlet bounced on a massive birthing ball with both hands on her back while Carlos paced the small length of the living room, phone pressed to his ear. The tiny studio apartment housed the whole of their lives in one room with only a separate space for the toilet and shower. Instead of a couch, a queen-size daybed doubled as a seating and sleeping spot and their TV balanced on a hand-me-down kitchen table from mine and Kai's condo. The kitchen lined one wall with a small sink, half-size refrigerator, and open shelving instead of cabinets.

I closed the door and slipped off my wet shoes. At the sound, Scarlet looked up.

"I think I'm dying," she said. Her porcelain milky skin was patched with red splotches, slick with sweat, and plastered with damp flyaway hairs from her messy bun.

"Will you let me take you to the hospital?" I asked. "Technically, your labor is coming early. Almost a month early which means you might need a doctor."

She shook her head and ran her palm over her face, dragging more frizzy hair into the sweat on her brow. "I lied."

The tension in my shoulders dropped and worry switched to instant irritation. I was too tired for lies.

"I can't do this at all," she said, blowing out a sigh. "I won't have this baby. I can't be a mom. I'll drop her or forget her on the bus or accidentally feed her honey. Did you know babies can't have honey?" Fear strained her voice as she looked up at me with wide emerald eyes. "What if I'm making tea and when I go to put honey in my mug, I'm so tired that I put it in her bottle and then it attracts a bee and she gets stung?"

"That's not how any of that works," I said with a wave of my hand. I took a seat on the daybed beside her birthing ball and gave her shoulder a gentle squeeze. "Okay, I lied too. Maybe the exhaustion you described and the mistakes you're afraid of are real. They happen and they suck."

Scarlet erupted into a groan that rivaled Jack's frustrated burbles. It seemed I'd gone from one angry baby to the next. Except Scar—the former Keeper of Stories and ancient being who'd existed across time and space, and had hunted and guided fairy tale characters to their deaths to keep the stories in place—had every right to cry. Motherhood was scary. Childbirth was scary. Hell, *life* in general was scary, and we'd seen some of the worst it had to offer—murders, villains, the devil himself from Hans Christian Andersen's *The Snow Queen*. I shuddered at the memory of Detective Wilhelm. He had revealed his true identity and demanded I give him the hood for the immortal properties it granted. Thankfully, Kai had taken him down, saving my life and stopping the corrupt detective from roaming the human world for eternity.

"BUT," I continued. "Mistakes are part of life. Isn't that what the themes and messages of stories tell us? We mess up and then we learn, and through it all we get to crack a few jokes."

Scarlet rolled her eyes and stopped bouncing. "For Kai maybe. And Wendy who has been picking up on her dad's jokes."

I laughed. "It's funny because it's true."

"But when you say something is funny after laughing it's not funny anymore," she said as deadpan as if we were talking about death and taxes.

I pretended to punch her arm and gave her a cheesy smile. "Hey, at least it distracted you. How far apart are contractions?"

"They stopped," she said, a blush blooming on her cheeks. "I figured out they were those fake labor, hickey things." As always, Scarlet refused to learn the correct name for things even though it'd be a breeze considering her impressive intelligence. She'd been assimilated into modern society for several years now. She'd even taken a paying job as a detective after doubling up on a rigorous internship while taking night classes at a community college to get her degree. Despite all of that, in times of high emotion or when she was relaxed around her closest friends, she still slipped into colloquialisms, pop culture phrases, cliches, and miswordings.

"Braxton Hicks contractions?" I nodded. "Good. Then you have plenty of time to practice mom life before game day."

"Game day?" Her brow wrinkled.

Carlos hung up the phone and padded across the cushy carpet. Remnants of his time as Pinocchio still slipped through in the stiff way he walked and the jerky movements of his neck. "My mom says you can't have the baby yet," he said. "She hasn't finished cooking and packaging our month's worth of freezer meals."

"Lucky," I muttered. My mom was a swan who'd flown away into the sky when I freed her from her possessive husband. I didn't get a single freezer meal from Jack's grandma when he was born for obvious reasons. After clearing my throat, I scooted to the edge of the daybed's cushion and laid my hand on Scar's shoulder. "As I was saying, practice makes perfect."

Scarlet used the dampness of her sweat to wipe flyaways from her face and plaster them against her greasy head. "You never said that."

"Look, I want to pitch an idea." Even as I said it, the thought of accepting the Grimm gods' call to go to Storyland sent goosebumps prickling my arms and neck. I didn't belong there. I belonged here in San Francisco, writing and reporting crimes and raising my two little nuggets. Scarlet's eyebrows peaked, and she tilted her head at me. "You need the practice as a mom and I need to figure out a way to seal the damn rift."

Scarlet cupped her massive belly with her palms and shot me a look of shock. "Curb your language, Lady. There are innocent ears here."

"Carlos is a real boy now, he can handle it," I said. They both shook their heads at me in perfect unison but I ignored their mild irritation. Making light of serious situations was my jam because it was the only way I could handle the intensity of life. If I took every villain, every dark story and crime lurking around the corner to heart, I'd suffer cardiac arrest before I hit menopause. "I'm going to cross over, through the rift. I have to continue Sherlock's studies to seal it or else…" my voice trailed.

"Or else you have to sacrifice yourself," she said.

I nodded. Scarlet, having been a version of Red Riding Hood once herself, knew how the story ended—a girl devoured by the wolf. She also knew I'd been studying the story under the Grimm gods' suggestion. And this is what made sense. It was Red's hood that held the magic. It was Red herself who existed across time and space to seal the stories, and though Scarlet couldn't remember her ancient life, she'd started somewhere and for some reason. When I'd stolen the hood from her, the torch had passed to me, nearly burning my entire life to the ground.

I smiled a grim smile and rubbed my eyes. "I was thinking you could take Jack and Wendy for me. That way you and Carlos could practice parenthood for a few days."

"Because Kai won't let you go alone," she said, reading me like a dang book.

"Because Kai won't let me go alone," I confirmed. We all knew that. He was the peanut butter to my banana sandwich—not jelly, because we were never exactly what others expected of us. Maybe he was more like the caramel sauce to my cheesecake. The Prince Charming to my Snow White. The Richard Castle to my Kate Beckett. John Winchester to my Mary—except I didn't die a horrific death and sentence my children to a life of hunting monsters. Not yet, anyway.

Scarlet offered me her sweaty hand to shake. "Deal. But if you're not back in time for my real labor, I'm going to murder you and you will be the first case I 'investigate' after maternity leave." With her free hand, she threw up air quotes to drive her point home.

I gave her a taste of her own medicine and rolled my eyes until it sparked a headache. *Not if the wolf murders me first.* If he devoured me, would the disasters stop? Would the rift finally seal and the story aura vanish from the human world?

Something about it—other than the obvious trauma of staring down my death—didn't feel right. I didn't belong in Storyland, so how could my murder right whatever had gone wrong with the story's reincarnation? I was a reporter, the one who wrote about crime, not the one involved in it.

I stood and stooped to give her a quick hug. "I'll bring the kids over after Wendy's play tomorrow."

"Don't die," she said. "I need you to help me raise Rapunzel."

"No promises, and no way in hell you're naming her that."

Carlos shook his head behind Scarlet's back and mouthed "*Definitely not.*"

I shuffled to the door and shoved my feet into the sneakers, still not bothering to tie them or pull the back of the shoe over my heels. At the door, I paused and tossed a last promise over my shoulder. "I can't die." I nodded to the TV that was playing a news channel. A newscaster warned viewers that the cannibal killer had not yet been apprehended—another wolf. "I have way too much work to do." *And way too much crime to report to keep this crazy city safe.*

Chapter Three

"True courage is in facing danger when you are afraid..."

— L. Frank Baum, The Wonderful Wizard of Oz

To passersby we likely resembled a crew of family and friends out for a mid-morning, Sunday stroll. In another life, Scarlet and I could be two sisters getting our steps in after a weekend brunch with our husbands and children.

If only our lives were so simple.

Someday, maybe I'd walk hand-in-hand with Kai while we watched our children bound ahead without a care in the world. Maybe we'd even get that dog Kai had been wanting. A poodle or a pug or a massive rescue breed like a Saint Bernard. Or we could adopt a Newfoundland to protect our children once I was...gone.

Lightning pain bolted through my chest as my heart skipped a beat. My eyes locked on the chubby grabby hand reaching out from the car seat that balanced atop a matching stroller.

If we didn't find a straightforward answer to close the rift, would I have to seal myself inside? Would I be bound to Red's story and forced to give myself over to the jaws of a reincarnating wolf as his crimson-hooded dinner? Either way, I was walking to the potential end of my story where I'd have to leave my children in order to save my children, along with hundreds of others of all ages.

This short winding walk that led to Pioneer Park could be my last. I resisted the sudden urge to glance back at San Francisco's towering buildings and busy streets full of car exhaust and Sunday shoppers. In another life, a vacation to Storyland where real magic and Cinderella existed could be an enchanting escape. But because of the fairy tale hell I had witnessed, I appreciated the mundanity of the human world. I appreciated the persistent honk of cars in a city teeming with life and purpose. I appreciated the hard, gray concrete beneath my feet that reminded me I stood on solid ground. I appreciated imperfections all around us from the stains on the bench where Kai and I had enjoyed many takeout dinner dates, to the shaggy curl of my husband's over-grown hair.

Feeling my gaze, Kai's neck twisted as he glanced over his shoulder. Concern darkened his pupils and creased his forehead but the ghost of a comforting smile crinkled at his tired eyes.

Wendy shuffled alongside her brother's stroller, sneakers dragging over the leaves that littered the concrete pathway. She was old enough to understand the truth that mommy and daddy were going far, far away in a land with stories from a long time ago. The weight of it tugged at her youthful innocence and childlike joy and her fears only furthered my resolve. It was time to end the threat and torment of fairy tales and villains once and for all. A child should be reading those stories for the themes that prepare one for the realities of life, not living through literal dark magic cast by evil witches.

Goosebumps pricked my arms and neck as a gust swept through the park. I tugged the collar of my peacoat up, missing the enchanted protection of Red's hood. If only I hadn't started to pull it away from the rift would we be fairy tale free? No. The Grimm gods liked to remind me that the hood's barrier always had a deadline. It was a Band-Aid on a broken bone, a squirt gun against a wildfire, a windbreaker in a hurricane.

*Speaking of a gun…*I patted the hostler wrapped around my belly, feeling for the hard weight of my 9mm. I'd met enough fairy tale monsters to know I needed to carry a precaution. Of course, I knew we were stepping into an entire world of villains and grim violence and that my little pistol might not be enough.

Carlos and Scarlet's steps followed behind us as the pathway opened to the park. To the right, a well-loved, brightly colored playground crouched over a shallow dip of rubber ground to pad the fall of clumsy children. A few benches were scattered along the path, some facing the kid's play area and others toward the concrete center. Tall lamp posts stood like sentinels around the large open center, ready to cast their protective glow against the dark of night. Pathways branched out from the concrete space, some into the forest for long walks or running trails, others led back out to the street.

In the dead center, a sheen of thin red fabric billowed in the breeze, suspended in mid-air and revealing a peek into Storyland. If you didn't know to look for it, the rift and its crimson bandage would resemble a falling leaf, or an odd shine of sunlight beaming through the crowd of tree branches overhead, or even a rust-colored puff of lingering smoke from a cigarette. But we knew exactly where to look for it, so the rip between realities was more of a glaring warning sign to me. *Stop* it seemed to say. *Danger Ahead.* Or perhaps, *No Trespassing, Restricted Area, May Cause Injury, Death, Or A Cliffhanger.*

Hey, at least with a cliffhanger it meant the story wasn't over. *My* story wasn't over.

"Can I take Jack down the slide?" Wendy asked, blinking up at me.

I scanned the park, noting a father with two young boys playing tag on the rubber flooring and a young woman bouncing a baby on her knee at a nearby bench. We'd need to wait for the area to clear out before we disappeared into the portal anyway so I nodded.

I jogged closer to the stroller to scoop the baby from his car seat cocoon. The young woman, a mom or possibly babysitter gaped at me as I passed Jack to Wendy. I pretended not to notice and avoided the urge to explain that my four-month-old had spent an impossible amount of time in the womb and alongside his winter magic; he was holding his head up at only two days old and he crawled by the time he was a month old. None of those enchanted developmental boosts made mothering him any easier. He still cried without explanation, struggled with spit up, and refused to sleep longer than two hours at a time.

Kai leaned close to me as we watched Wendy huff her oversized baby brother up the playground's steps. "You're coming home," he said.

My brows knitted together, and I met his gaze. "What if not coming home spares hundreds of children and innocent people for decades to come?"

A grim smile twisted his lips, but it quickly vanished, and he shook his head. "Nah. I don't believe feeding yourself to a reincarnating wolf is the answer. You've always found a way to stay safe in the face of danger. Did you forget why you became an investigative journalist?"

My eyes flicked back to the play structure. Both Jack and Wendy squealed happily as she snuggled him into her lap and launched them down the slide together. "Reporting danger isn't just for me. It's for keeping others safe too."

"I know," Kai said, voice low. He looped his arm around my shoulder and tugged me closer, inviting me to rest my head on him. "But I believe you can do both."

Both? Save myself and the rest of the freaking world? Talk about pressure. But the crushing weight of it didn't settle over my lungs. Despite the situation, an odd rush of encouragement fluttered in my chest. If the wolf reincarnated, and I was truly Red now, could I rein-carnate too? Could I let him eat me in this world only to exist again in Storyland? And if so, maybe sealing the rift wasn't the answer—not yet, anyway. I could end the story and escape through the opening. Still, that didn't seal the rip between realities. I could hear the Grimm gods now... *Oh, your basic human mind is precious. This is a world of gods and immortality and story where the climax is ever so much more than one simple answer.*

"A world of gods," I muttered. Was every narrator a god in Story-land? A creator reincarnating with the spawn of their stories?

"What's up?" Kai said, drawing his attention from the kids.

"I was just saying that you're such a sap," I teased, trying to lighten the mood. "Or is it just that you can't handle Wendy and Jack without me?"

He bumped me with his elbow. "Hey, I was the one who got Wendy ready for her play this morning *and* got her there on time."

"And for that, I am eternally grateful," I said with an honest smile. The opportunity to watch our daughter's performance at her school theater's final showing was the perfect sendoff before we crossed through the rift. Wendy had radiated confidence and power on the stage as she spoke the words written by James Matthew Barrie so long ago. Somehow, I'd had the words memorized too. I'd whispered them before she bellowed the script aloud. Of course I'd read *Peter Pan* before and was present while she practiced for the play, but it was more than that. I remembered the quotes with a different word here and there. I saw the text in my mind's eye with sections crossed out and rewritten almost as if I were Barrie himself, toiling over the manuscript.

That was what too much stress and too little sleep did to my brain. Stress turned into nightmares of writing a novel when I was a reporter at heart. I didn't create characters; I aided real human lives with my words through journalism.

Scarlet and Carlos stepped into the play area, Carlos offered to help Wendy reach the monkey bars and Scarlet scooped Jack into her arms.

"See?" I raised my voice. "You're already killing it at this mom thing."

Scarlet rolled her eyes and balanced Jack on her hip. The fact that he obliterated size charts for his age was painfully obvious against her slight frame. Scarlet was wiry but smaller than me and even carrying her heavy belly, she didn't struggle with Jack's weight the way I did. She was already a stronger mom than me.

"That's only because your kids are unusually tough," she said. "I bet I'll break mine."

I winced. She wasn't wrong. My kids had been through a winter storm and came out on the other side more resilient than ever. Wendy had survived the story aura's pull as Peter Pan, her mother turning into a vampire, and her father's moody behavior when he'd fallen prey to his role as Kai from Hans Christian Andersen's *The Snow Queen*.

"Practice starts now," I said to Scarlet with a little wave. I tilted my head to the bench I'd claimed as mine. I laced my fingers through Kais and tugged him toward our spot. Once we took a seat, I didn't mince words. "Are you sure you want to come?"

"With you? Always," he said, a mischievous spark in his eye. "It will be an adventure that we tell our grandkids about."

I left it at that. I could do this alone, but I didn't want to. It may have only been a distant dream from a nightmare long ago, but I had the memory that I'd done this before. I'd crossed realms and worlds, if only in my imagination.

I nestled my head on his shoulder and we listened to the sounds of happy children. After a moment of rest, we joined in, racing in a game of tag and playing hide and seek until Wendy announced she was hungry.

That was our cue.

"Take her to The Girled Cheese," I said, referring to the hole-in-the-wall grilled cheese restaurant run by two sisters. "It's her favorite."

"I know," Scarlet said as we all shuffled closer to the center of Pioneer Park. "You act as if I haven't babysat her a hundred times before."

"I was only a phone call away then." I glanced at the rift, the hood, the scrap of fabric whipping in the wind.

She followed my gaze and said, "you already figured out that the hood and the rift are made of the same magic, this can't be much harder."

Heat crawled up my neck. Was I blushing? "Dang. Why is everyone so confident in me? I don't know if I can handle the pressure." I tried to laugh, but it came out as a croak, heavy with emotion.

"Because you're literally the only person to have ever thought to twist your story's ending *and* steal the hood in the history of stories," she said, her voice deadpan to emphasize the obvious. "That has to mean something. You weren't just a human-turned-character like the rest, not with an idea like that."

I could almost feel the Grimm gods chuckling. They'd probably insist humans didn't have ideas—not real ones, unless they were authors. A soft scoff escaped me as we approached the rift.

"Well." I sighed. "Let's see what the hell kind of magic is on the other side." And if I had any clue how to seal it.

We stopped in front of the rift and I peeled the torn fabric away to reveal a glimpse into Storyland. Jagged mountains rose and fell in the distance where dark clouds shadowed their peaks. In a straight line, the world was split, the weather entirely different with an impossibly blue sky and brilliant emerald hills. I squinted at the sight of shimmering yellow on the ground, a trail of shiny golden flowers—no, was it brick?

I turned to face Scarlet and Carlos and Wendy and Jack, finally ready to say our goodbyes.

"Have fun storming the alternate-universe castles," Scarlet said with a sly smile.

I kissed Jack's forehead and placed him back into Scarlet's arms before crouching to pull Wendy into a hug. "We hope to be back soon, Wednesday." I called her by her nickname as I held tightly, pressing her into me so she couldn't see the tears swimming in my eyes. The usual smell of Goldfish cheese crackers and fruit-scented markers wafted from her, the aromatic mark of her starving artist personality.

"Are you fixing a story?" she asked as she pulled back.

"We're fixing the portal. Closing it if we can."

The freckles on her nose danced as she scrunched her face, considering this. "So there will be no more villains?"

"That's what we're hoping for," I said.

She shrugged. "I'd just write the story without bad guys."

I laughed. "That's a genius idea. Can you write one with Auntie Scar's help so I can read it when I get back?"

With a nod, she sealed the deal and then threw herself into me for another hug. We all exchanged goodbyes and *I love yous* until my throat squeezed so tightly I couldn't speak. I gasped for one last breath of San Francisco air before lifting my foot and planting it on the other side.

Unlike the solid concrete of Pioneer Park, Storyland's unsteady ground rumbled beneath me and I was already falling.

Chapter Four

"Trip away; make no stay."

— William Shakespeare, A Midsummer Night's
Dream

A shock radiated through my elbow as I hit the road. The view from inside Storyland provided clarity. Now that I was closer, I saw the line between stories blurring, the storm clouds from *Wuthering Heights* passed over into the bright hills of *Pride and Prejudice's* England in springtime. The distance was hard to calculate here as if the space itself wobbled between measurements.

Wind whipped hair into my face and mouth. Strands that had escaped from my low ponytail wrapped around my throat, choking me. In the distance, clouds swirled together in a funnel and dipped down to touch the ground with a violent embrace. A tornado.

My hand went to my only source of protection, but a pistol was useless against the tornado that tore through Storyland. It shredded through the neon colors of Wonderland and ripped towering trees from the ground in a forest-laden fairy tale—possibly the same forest where Red encountered the wolf. My heart slammed into my stomach and I released my useless, white-knuckled grip on the weapon beneath my shirt.

A movement drew my eyes from the impending threat to the rift. Kai emerged from the other side, gripping the edge of the portal itself and his knuckles went white as he held the pulsing magic. He reached out to help me up and our fingers grazed before the rumbling earth knocked him on top of me. His wrist hit the brick beneath us as he managed a quick roll to avoid crushing me.

The swirling column of dust and debris barreled toward us, picking up cows and Cheshire Cats and…was that a house? A complete home with cute little shutters and a front porch went round and round. A woman with a tall, pointed hat stood resolute at the base of the tornado, unmoving, unafraid while a creature shaped like a gingerbread man ran away from the storm. The wind tore gumdrops and icing off of his body, stripping him naked as he raced for safety toward a small house made of the same material as his skin.

As if pulled by an invisible string, the tornado followed his path. The swirling cow dipped from the wind's hold, just close enough for the cow to nip at the gingerbread man's head, taking a chunk right out of his skull.

A laugh bubbled out of me. A. *Laugh*. What in the fairy tale hell had we stepped into?

Kai yanked on my arm as he scrambled to his feet. "We have to run!" he shouted.

I couldn't move, couldn't think. I could do nothing but laugh at the absurdity of the cow getting a Christmas-flavored snack before the tornado threw it across stories where the mooing creature landed on a springy, plush mushroom in an untouched area of Wonderland.

Frozen in place, I let Kai drag me off the brick road and into congealed cold mud. The chill rippled through me, jolting sense into me. I clutched his forearm but we couldn't get to our feet with the intensity of the storm's wind. If the tornado swept us up, we likely wouldn't get the same good luck as the cow.

All at once, the tornado vanished and the flying house landed on top of the gingerbread man's shelter, crushing it into oblivion. Maybe the Christmas cookie's luck wasn't so good after all.

Relief rushed out of me in a sigh and I went limp, dropping my head into the soil-turned-sludge. Not even two minutes inside Storyland and our lives had already been threatened. Was this the worst decision of my life? Probably.

An echoing cackle bounced off of the hills behind us. I pulled my head from the suctioning mud in time to see the woman disappear behind the rubble.

"Was that..." Kai started, pointing at where the woman had stood. "The witch from *Hansel and Gretel*?" A note of fear quivered in his voice, likely at the memory of the witch who had hunted him during the winter storm only a few months before. "Or wait, *Rapunzel*? What about *Sleeping Beauty*? *Snow White*?"

"Oz," I breathed. "She was the Wicked Witch of the East." How did I know that? The information had landed in my brain suddenly and in the same way Dorothy's Kansas house landed on top of the gingerbread man. I didn't wear the hood, and I wasn't really The Keeper of Stories. So what gave me the confidence that I was right about this? I silently blamed Scarlet and Kai who had both filled my head with too much nonsensical praise.

"The *what*?" His hair hung in his eyes as he looked back and forth between me and Dorothy's house. "I thought the Wicked Witch of the West was the antagonist."

"Her too," I said. "The east witch wasn't supposed to survive. In *The Wonderful Wizard of Oz* Dorothy's house lands on top of the east witch, killing her instantly."

He pointed at the house. "And you're sure..."

I nodded. "I'm sure she's the east witch. And I'm sure the stories are royally and completely screwed up."

I bent forward and plucked a lively daisy straight out of the sinking mud. None of this made sense but the Grimm gods' fear was suddenly clearer than the ice pebbles I'd find in Jack's diaper. Storyland was more than a mess, it was dangerous and it was spilling over into San Francisco.

I squeezed my eyes shut and thought of Wendy's suggestion. *Write the story without the bad guys.* If only I could fix this all with the swipe of ink on the page. If only I could cross out the errors and rewrite the cow back into *Jack and the Beanstalk* instead of where he now stood munching on the mushroom in Wonderland.

Finally, I peeled my eyes open and stood, following Kai to the rift. Despite the chaos that had just unfolded before us, we had to stay focused. A few flying cows and murdered gingerbread men couldn't distract me from my mission to fix the fairy tales and end the suffering.

Mud squashed beneath my feet until I stepped back onto the glittering brick road and approached the rift.

The rip in the middle of the world was unrecognizable from this side. Instead of a red hood threaded into the living magic, it looked like a jagged scar suspended in mid-air. I reached out and touched the material on the rift's edge only to find it was nothing like the pulsing, fleshy substance that existed in Pioneer Park.

I rubbed the dry, creased paper edge between my thumb and forefinger. It felt no different from the well-loved and worn pages of a book in the San Francisco library. On an urge, I leaned forward and took a whiff of the rift's smell. As suspected, my nose filled with the sweet, musty scent of old novels.

Kai's brows knitted together, and he gave me a lopsided smile riddled with confusion. "Are we sniffing for clues now?"

"Try it," I suggested, gesturing to the torn edge. "It smells just like an old bookstore."

"Mmhmm." He hummed as he dipped forward and sniffed. "That or you're actually the wolf instead of Red."

I rolled my eyes. "Yeah, didn't you know? I'm the werewolf mom from that cozy mystery series who can smell people's emotions."

"*Magic, Movies, and Murder?*" He asked. "The one I bought you for Christmas right?"

I nodded, recalling the 1990s amateur sleuth series called *Bewitcher's Beach*. Kai had given it to me hoping the cozy atmosphere combined with the murder investigation would both help me relax and keep my interest. He'd been right.

If I were an author, I'd write stories like that—always a happy ending with a little intrigue. No tales about little red-hooded girls getting devoured by monstrous beasts. I brushed my fingertips against the rift's paper until the thin edge sliced the soft flesh of my thumb. I yanked my hand back and sucked the blood from the stinging wound.

"Did you see that?" Kai asked. He squinted at the edge and gingerly pulled back the paper to reveal more pages beneath. The rift was layered with dozens—no hundreds, thousands—of pages beneath the first.

I groaned. Studying the rift's magic was going to take a lot longer than I'd thought. Billions of words must have been crammed into the pages that layered the rift.

"What kind of magic is this?" I breathed. Despite the paper cut, I reached out again and touched the pages, too curious and impatient to wait for the bleeding to stop.

A bead of red stained the paper's edge and bled through the pages in veiny lines. Kai gasped and peeled back more pages. My blood snaked across the paper leaving thousands of thin red strikes through words, sentences, and sometimes whole pages. Kai's knuckles turned white as he pulled harder to reveal more of the pages. We both watched, speechless with awe, horror, and confusion. Occasionally, the red would fill in the blank space with big bold letters. Some notes were simple words like *remove* or *add more description*, but others seemed sucked straight out of my brain. One note read: *what in the Wonderland does this mean?* Another said *this is fairy tale hell, rewrite!*

"Is it—" I swallowed and paused to find the words. "Is my blood editing the rift?"

Chapter Five

"Experience is the only thing that brings knowledge, and the longer you are on earth the more experience you are sure to get."

— L. Frank Baum, The Wonderful Wizard of Oz

Kai slowly turned his head, only raising his eyebrows in response to my outlandish question. The blood from my paper-cut stained the pages inside the rift. As if it had a life of its own, the stain swirled and looped around words, making notes while it spread.

With a grunt, Kai released the pages and flexed his fingers before pinching the rift's edge again. As he fanned through the papers, a big red splotch caught my eye.

"Stop!" My hand shot out. "I saw something. Go back a few... hundred pages." How big was this book? Was it a collection of all the tales in Storyland? I snorted at the thought of this alternate world's atmosphere comprising literal stories. Because why not? What did I expect? An actual scientific explanation for the rift? For the magic to comprise clues like a murder investigation? I'd just watched Dorothy's house slaughter a gingerbread man and Jack's cow enjoy a mushroom from Wonderland. Why would the rift itself be any less wild and confusing? "If only good ol' Sherlock Holmes had left us some clues."

Kai clucked his tongue and then spoke while still fanning through the pages. "He was a genius, but none of his cases involved magic."

"True." I sighed. If a genius from one of this world's stories couldn't solve the mystery of the rift's magic, how could I?

Finally, Kai found the page with the circle of red. The editor's note —AKA my blood—circled one word one dozen times, *Oz*.

"What does it mean?" Kai asked, glancing at me and the page.

I stepped closer and squinted at the veiny line that trailed away from the circle. "Follow that thread," I said. He carefully turned the pages, where the line continued through the bottom margin. It almost reminded me of a thin red string used on an investigation board. And I almost expected a thumbtack stuck to the spot where it stopped. The trail finally ended at another circled word. "Wardrobe," I read. The blood ink had connected both *Wardrobe* and *Oz*.

"And what does that mean?" Kai asked again. "Dorothy wants new clothes? Or does the wizard?"

I shook my head. "I don't know but it's connecting *The Lion, The Witch, and the Wardrobe* with *The Wonderful Wizard of Oz*." My breath caught in my throat as the red streamed over the page again. "It's still going," I said, pointing to the jagged line. It snaked between words and over pages until it circled a pair of words before moving on again. *Oz. Wardrobe. Rabbit hole.*

"From *Alice in Wonderland*," Kai said, noting the story where the rabbit hole was found.

The blood trail continued as if my life force was an all-powerful editor. I frowned at the thought. What had made me so different from all the other characters Scarlet and I had encountered? Why was I the only one who successfully thwarted the sad ending of my fairy tale's tragedy? And most importantly, why did my blood look like red ink as it circled two phrases in *A Midsummer Night's Dream?*

...steep themselves in night.

...dream away the time.

The editing stopped. No more trail. A dead end of blood ink with a collection of confusing words.

"Steep themselves in night and dream away the time," Kai read aloud, his voice breathy and already tired. His free hand raked through his hair with spread fingers. He said the last two circled phrases several more times while I wracked my brain for ideas. "Maybe they're all dreams? Did Alice dream of Wonderland?"

I folded my arms, and my frown deepened. "Not quite. And why would the whole phrase be circled and not just the word 'dream'?"

He hummed and then said, "good point."

My gaze fell to my feet, unseeing as I stared at a blur of yellow on the ground and mused over the collection of words. "Each of those stories has a secondary world right?"

"You mean like an alternate universe?"

I nodded and tapped my finger to my lips. "Oz. Narnia. Wonderland. And…the fairy realm for *A Midsummer Night's Dream*?" I peeled my gaze from the yellow brick and looked at Kai.

"That sounds right to me, but you're the story expert."

"Story Keeper," I mumbled. "And not anymore. Wait!" A thought formed, slow but steady and nothing like the bolt of lightning that had instantly helped me identify the Wicked Witch of the East. This time I had control over my mind and the sudden information didn't overwhelm or confuse me. I worked through the speculation that the red notes intended to highlight the portals in each story. "In *The Lion, The Witch, and The Wardrobe*, the kids enter Narnia through the wardrobe."

"Interesting," Kai said. The eager look in his eyes prodded me to continue.

"The rabbit hole is how Alice gets to Wonderland. Those are both portals and the rift itself is a portal. Could the words be referring to the rift's magic? I just can't figure out how Oz and those lines from *A Midsummer Night's Dream* fit in." Frustration bubbled in my stomach. Or maybe the grumbling came from the lack of brunch I could have enjoyed if I lived an alternate, quiet life.

Kai repeated Shakespeare's lines again. The comedic play didn't match the other stories. After a moment, he snapped his fingers. "But you dream when you sleep and 'steeping yourself in night' could refer to sleep as well. Dreams are almost like a secondary world and sleep is how you get to them."

"You're saying sleep is a portal?" That answered how Shakespeare's play fit in with the latter three stories. Was sleep considered a portal in *The Wonderful Wizard of Oz*? I tried to recall the details of Dorothy falling asleep while the tornado carried her house around. Or was the tornado the portal?

Frazzled hair bobbed over his eyes as he nodded. A grin spread across Kai's face. "This is kind of fun."

A huff escaped me. "I'd much rather be stewing at my spot on the couch with a Cheesecake Factory order on my lap and a good show to binge."

He shrugged. "The adventures are keeping us young."

"Speak for yourself." I yawned. "It's past my bedtime and my brain cannot connect Oz to these portal stories. Maybe if I go to sleep, I'll dream up the answer." Another lightning bolt shot through my head. The intense overlap of information beat like a painful pulse in my temples. *I wrote these notes.* Somewhere and at some point, I had sat down with these books and a red marker and circled the words. The memory was as clear as day with an image in my mind's eye. I saw my hand pinching a ballpoint pen. The tip tapped against the page where it read *"Oz himself is the Great Wizard"*.

"Mari?" Kai's gentle voice eased me from the vision and my brain stopped radiating with pain. The image of the memory vanished in a pop and all the tension melted away. "Are you okay?"

"Headache," I said, my voice raspy. "But I figured it out. I think."

"Yeah?"

I smiled a grim smile. "The Wizard of Oz must know how the portals work. He's the only circled word that isn't a gateway to another world. For some reason, the notes connect him with the portals of the other stories, which means he might understand the magic of *this* portal." My fingertip brushed against the flat page where Kai still held it open to *A Midsummer Night's Dream*. The bleeding on my fingertip had stopped and the cut already healed as if it had never been. I didn't question it. At least I wouldn't need a bandage *and* painkillers now. Though the headache had subsided, I sensed that the lightning bolt of memories and information wasn't over yet. Maybe my time as a Keeper of Stories had taught me more than I'd thought.

"If our buddy the Wizard of Oz knows about portals, does that mean he's got tools in his magic kit to fix this one?" Kai asked. He finally shut the book inside the rift.

"Maybe. It's a long shot. A guess, really, but I hope it's right because my brain is out of commission until I down a bottle of aspirin and sleep for a week."

Kai reached for my hand, lacing his fingers through mine. He gently tugged me along. "Then let's find this dude and hire him ASAP. I assume the yellow brick road is our best bet?"

I blinked at the road that was too bright to look at after the migraine left my eyes weak. Without answering, I squeezed his hand and fell into place beside him. I kept pace with him, matching him step for step despite the urge to turn, run, and dive back through the rift to safety on the other side.

After miles, or minutes, or maybe acres, my calves burned. The road wound on and on in a seemingly endless trail of glittering yellow. It was impossible to determine how far we'd walked since the world ebbed and flowed around us as if the horizon stretched of its own accord.

The stories' settings swirled around us, bleeding into one another like the red on the page. Characters approached the yellow brick road but most were too distracted to notice us. A woman I knew as Elizabeth Bennet from *Pride and Prejudice* argued with a man who certainly wasn't Mr. Darcy. I slowed to squint at the target of her disagreement until I recognized him as Jay Gatsby, the wealthy young man from F. Scott Fitzgerald's *The Great Gatsby*.

I tore my gaze away, trying to stay focused on the road to the Wizard of Oz but a squeal from my left pulled my attention. A rippling ocean stood right in the middle of a meadow. The waves crashed against the base of a tall stone tower, weakening the building's frame with every splash. The tower's pointed tip swayed as the base below wobbled.

A shimmering scaly tail slapped against the water until another wave lifted the sea creature and dashed its body against the stones. I gasped as the wave subsided, revealing a very dead little mermaid.

"Keep going," Kai said, the voice of reason. It took all of my strength to ignore the three goats charging a young and frightened princess who ran barefoot through the snow. The Billy goats trampled a glass slipper beneath their hooves, shattering the shoe into a million shards.

"I can save her," I said, but Kai squeezed my fingers tighter.

"Yes, you can, when we commission our good ol' Oz guy to fix the rift."

I nodded slowly as if in a stupor. Watching fairy tales at war twisted my gut. My stomach turned sour, and a weight pressed on my chest. I wanted to rescue Cinderella and stop Grendel, *Beowulf's* villain, from kissing the sleeping beauty. It hurt to ignore it, to walk by and do nothing. But it'd hurt a lot worse to get stuck here, eternally trying to undo what the broken world had set at war. I'd never catch up, never be able to stop the bleeding between stories until I found the answer to heal the rift. And I'd never see my children again if I gave in to join the surrounding battles.

Still, the pain both emotional and mental, beat in my head and heart, and every muscle in my tense body only pulsed and worsened with each step.

At least, if nothing else, I had my husband's hand to hold. I gripped harder and let him pull me along through an indeterminate space across indeterminate time. How long ago had our Storyland adventure begun? Did I fall through the rift seconds ago or had months passed? Had Scarlet already given birth? Were my children okay? After crossing through another battle between *Treasure Island's* pirates and Louisa May Alcott's *Little Women*, we finally stopped in front of a palace.

Kai released his hold and offered me the best smile he could muster. "Welcome to Emerald City, I guess."

Chapter Six

"Do you think Oz could give me courage?"

— L. Frank Baum, The Wonderful Wizard of Oz

The shimmering green palace encompassed all of my attention. Despite the lack of sunlight, every peak beamed bright as if the towers' jagged tips had impaled a fallen star. The glassy surface looked fragile, as if it'd shatter to the touch. If it were blue, it might have been made by cartoon Elsa, but the frosty emerald shade identified this palace as belonging to L. Frank Baum's *The Wonderful Wizard of Oz*.

Though impressive, the palace bore scars of the war raging in Storyland. Cracks splintered through several walls. Chunks were missing from the steps that led to the double door. A wooden board was nailed across the doors but a broken gap revealed a glimpse inside.

We floated up the steps in a trance with our eyes glued to the graffiti on the wooden board. *Keep out! That means you, Oberon!*

"Oberon?" I breathed the first word spoken since Kai had announced our arrival to Emerald City.

"Who is that?" Kai asked. I felt his gaze ping-pong from the graffiti to me and back again.

"Oberon is the king of the fairies from *A Midsummer Night's Dream*," I said. "In the story, he and his wife Titania argue over a child. When Oberon gets mad, he tries to humiliate Titania by having his servant Puck give her a potion that makes her fall in love with a donkey."

"What an a—"

"Go away!" A shout interrupted Kai's inappropriate comment. The squeaky voice echoed against the walls inside the palace. "I'm not interested in helping you with your stupid fairy feud!"

The sound of defeat and fear didn't match the image I had of the all-powerful wizard. But this was the Wizard of Oz's palace and I suddenly knew that he was the source of the voice.

"Wizard of Oz!" I said, projecting my voice through the gap in the doors.

Silence.

I exchanged a glance with Kai and repeated the wizard's name, louder this time. After a moment, shuffling footsteps slid across the floor. I peered through the gap but saw no sign of life or movement inside.

"Is—is that you, Titania?" he asked.

Kai arched an eyebrow, and I shrugged. Maybe the lightning headaches had provided information before, but I was migraine-free and clueless about this situation. Why did the Wizard of Oz care about the queen of the fairies?

"Have you returned..." his voice trailed off, but when he spoke again, it sounded closer. "Are you back from Boredom?"

"Boredom?" Kai whispered. I waved for him to shush and then turned to look through the crack between the doors.

A gasp caught in my throat at the sight of an oversized eyeball staring back at me. My hand went to the 9mm around my waist while I kept my gaze locked. The massive brown eye bulged from wrinkled skin that seemed barely able to hold the eyeball in place. It shifted, looking me up and down as if it was the Eye of Sauron and had spotted Frodo on the mountain.

When the Wizard of Oz moved away from the door, I saw he was nothing more than a disembodied head floating in mid-air. With a sickening pop, the head burst into flames. The Wizard of Oz became a ball of fire, still suspended above ground as the blaze cracked and licked with an insatiable hunger. The entire scene should have jarred me, but I knew I wasn't hallucinating, and this wasn't a horror story.

The shiver that rippled through me quickly melted. Resolve tensed in my muscles and I refused to back away from the gap in the doors. After having read *The Wonderful Wizard of Oz,* I knew the ball of fire, the floating head, and the disembodied voice were nothing but tricks played by a powerful master of magic. According to the book, he was nothing more than an ordinary man—a circus magician, in fact.

"You don't scare me," I said.

The ball of fire flickered. The flames stretched and spread as blazing limbs formed. Arms and legs and a head grew until the fire vanished, leaving behind charred remains of a monster with a midnight black mouth and hollow unseeing eyes. Smoke billowed from its jagged jaws.

"You. Don't. Scare. Me." I repeated through gritted teeth. The monster's mouth opened, opened, opened until it seemed it'd swallow the palace itself. I clung to the memory of L. Frank Baum's novel. *He's just a man. Just a conman. Just a silly circus magician.*

"Mari…" Kai touched my shoulder. I twisted my neck to the side to see if his expression matched the horror in his voice. As expected, he saw the monster through the gap and the image had frozen him in fear.

"It's all smoke and mirrors," I whispered, my voice raspy. "It's not real." I said it as much for myself as I did to comfort my husband. Turning back to the Wizard of Oz, I forced power into my tone and raised the volume. "My name is Mari Fable and I'm here because of the rift between Storyland and the human world."

Silence.

The monster stood speechless and unmoving. His jaw stopped spreading open and in the blink of an eye, the terrifying creature vanished.

In its place stood a short, bald man with sharp eyebrows and a curious countenance. Wrinkles creased his mouth and forehead. Instead of an expanding mouth, it was his eyes that widened and widened and widened.

"Um," I continued. "I'm hoping you know more about the magic of the rift. The—uh—portal between our worlds."

He didn't so much as blink. Why was he just staring up at me like I was a celebrity and he was an awestruck fanboy? The Wizard of Oz finally shuffled forward. Before I could gather my thoughts, he yanked on the doors with surprising strength. The wooden board splintered inward, splitting apart in the center. It broke open as the doors spread wider.

Without a word, the Wizard of Oz gestured for us to enter.

I glanced at Kai before stepping across the palace's threshold. Silently, we followed in the wizard's wake until we stood beneath a crystal chandelier that sent sparkles darting around the grand entryway. The palace was cold and stark, void of life and furniture and hope. The Wizard of Oz himself walked with a defeated stoop as if hope had been sucked from his soul. But when he stopped and turned to me, his eyes brightened and the mood lifted.

"I've always wanted to meet an author," he said.

"A what?" I asked. I tilted my head with my ear closer to him.

"An author," he repeated, as if the single word clarified everything. After a moment of blinking and shifting gazes, he opened his mouth. "You're from the human world, yes?"

We nodded.

His focus dropped to his feet, and his voice followed, dipping into a mutter. "Maybe she can help Oberon and I'll get that dang fairy off my back."

"Excuse me," I said. "Why did you call me an author?" I couldn't get the thought out of my mind. I wasn't a writer, but maybe the work I'd done as The Keeper of Stories was considered editing for the stories. The Wizard of Oz's vision of me almost matched the unexplained memory of when I'd stooped over a manuscript with a red pen.

"Because you are from where the stories are made," he said as he beamed up at me. "The authors live in the human world."

"What about him?" I pointed to Kai, hoping to get the short man's glued gaze off of me again. "Believe it or not, he's also human."

"Hey!"

I bit back a smirk.

The Wizard of Oz gave Kai a once over before he returned his wide-eyed admiration to me. "Curious," he said. "But I suppose not everyone in the human world is an author."

"Hey!" Kai repeated. "I'll have you know, I wrote half a screenplay once." He pointed at the Wizard of Oz, pinning the magician with his gaze. "It was about an immortal history professor. Think Doctor Who but cooler."

"Nothing is cooler than Doctor Who," I deadpanned.

"Tell that to Buffy," he said with an exaggerated scoff.

"The rift," the Wizard of Oz said, interrupting our stupid banter. Sure it was inappropriate timing for a playful dispute over TV shows, but that was how Kai comforted me. We had to joke because if we didn't, we'd wonder about our children's safety. We'd consider the possibility that I'd have to sacrifice myself to the wolf. We'd be nothing but two clueless humans in a strange and dangerous world amid an unending war. "Are you here to fix it?"

"Yes. Did the Grimm gods tell you that?" I asked.

Confusion flickered over his face. He shook his head. "I know of no gods other than those written into mythologies."

I glanced at Kai and then back to the Wizard of Oz. "Jacob and Wilhelm Grimm. They're authors of famous fairy tales. Many of the same tales that I've seen just on my walk here to Emerald City. You have to know who I'm talking about if you know of human authors."

The Wizard of Oz cocked his head. "I know what they do but not who they are. Not beyond a mere name, anyway, which I believe is simply a pseudonym for a single writer. Deep within, every character knows we are the creations of imagination. Even so, we are not acquainted with those who imagine us. Authors do not come to Oz—or author, singular—if you are to believe what Sherlock Holmes uncovered during his investigation."

My heart jumped at the mention of Holmes's name. Even the word 'investigation' sent eager chills down my spine and settled in my stomach with fluttering excitement. Now the Wizard of Oz was talking in my language. "What did he uncover?"

The wizard sniffed and lifted his head, squinting at the glittering chandelier. Its glow bounced off of his shiny skull like a lit beacon. "The handwriting. Sherlock Holmes said all the manuscripts' handwriting matched. If you're as sharp as me and Holmes, you'll realize that this discovery suggests a single author for all stories. L. Frank Baum could have been the same person as Charlotte Bronte. So on and so forth. Of course it's not always as simple as handwriting. Holmes theorized the author didn't always create stories the same way, not everything was written in the style of a story. Some manuscripts are records of spoken words passed from mouth to mouth, some are plays meant to be performed, others are epic poems." He gestured at nothing with his hands. I almost expected another magic trick, but no monster or ball of fire appeared.

When he fell silent, I tried to wrap my mind around the concept. If that were true, the stories themselves weren't the only things reincarnating. Authors throughout time and history would be the reincarnation of a singular being.

"Like Doctor Who," I mumbled.

"Because of the—" Kai met my gaze and spun his finger. I knew he was reading my mind and taking the words right out of my head.

"Because of the reincarnation." I nodded. "Yeah."

He snapped his fingers. "Dang. I guess it *is* cooler than Buffy if you consider that side of it."

I ignored the bait to banter again and focused on the magician. The Wizard of Oz seemed lost in his own mind, possibly musing over the concept of one singular author. If he believed that, it made sense why he'd stared at me with awe. Apparently, he saw me as the creator of all stories across time and space. He thought I was a writer who breathed life into the thousands of living, breathing characters in Storyland.

Weird. But also kind of cool. I'd never liked the idea of being immortal before, but if I could compare myself to Doctor Who, it'd make the concept more agreeable. Too bad I was just an investigative journalist from San Francisco who had stumbled into the world of fairy tales. *No Time Lord or god-like author here.*

"Did Sherlock Holmes uncover anything else? Maybe a way to fix the rift between our worlds?"

The Wizard of Oz's gaze dropped from the chandelier. He blinked at me before squeezing his eyes shut. "No." His voice cracked with the same defeat and fear I'd heard in him earlier. When he spoke again, his tone came out shaky and his eyes were filled with tears. "I had so much hope that he'd heal what I had destroyed."

"You?" Kai and I both said it at the same time.

He nodded slowly as sadness deepened the wrinkles around his mouth and quivering chin. After a moment of silence, he sucked in a breath as if preparing to perform a long poem. "If you must know it was once upon a time when a human girl was sent to Storyland by… well, by the author. At least that is what I've come to understand since the authors are the only ones with enough power. Something happened, and I became confused. I thought the girl was Dorothy because no other young girls had existed in *The Wonderful Wizard of Oz* before. Now that I am wiser, I know she was not Dorothy. She did not belong here, and that was why she could cross story boundaries."

"Older, wiser, not to mention reincarnated about a million times," Kai muttered under his breath. I shot him a look with furrowed brows, but quickly relented because he was right to mention reincarnation…

I turned to the wizard again. "How is it that you can remember all of this? And Sherlock too when your story should have started over?"

He rubbed a hand over his bald head and blinked rapidly. "Because of the influence of the authors' world, the characters are evolving. Slowly but surely we all learn and understand, but each at our own pace, Ma'am."

I frowned at 'Ma'am' because it made me sound ancient. Kai leaned close with a smirk on his face and whispered a reassurance in my ear. "I know what you're thinking and no—you do not look old."

The Wizard of Oz didn't notice the exchange, too distracted by the story he was telling. As soon as he continued, I found myself engrossed as well. "The poor child had been lost in the woods when she came across Emerald City wearing only a thin red cloak to protect her against the elements. She told me she was waiting for her parents but since I mistook her for Dorothy, I did what my story said to do."

"Which is?" Kai prodded.

We both shot him an irritated look, and he raised his hands in surrender. I wanted him to shush so I could hear every detail about the girl in the woods—the girl who must have been Red Riding Hood. Or a version of her. How had she come from the human world and taken the place as a character?

"I told her she must kill the Wicked Witch of the West before I could help her."

I let the information sink in, slowly processing the fact that this wizard had guided Red to murder a witch rather than follow her story and meet the wolf at her grandmother's house.

The Wizard of Oz continued. "Storyland has never been the same. The tales eroded first with only subplots and minor characters here and there. Then the twists and errors built upon one another affecting protagonists and villains. Even entire settings. Characters went missing and plots were dropped. Endings never came and climaxes fell flat." A sigh escaped him and his bony shoulders sagged. "All because I was confused and the girl who was not Dorothy did not know how to kill the witch. Nor did she want to, I suppose, since she outright refused. When the witch was not melted by Dorothy's bucket of water, my story's plot experienced its first error."

"Did this girl go by Red Riding Hood? Or simply Red?" I asked.

He shook his head, and the top of his skull caught the shine of the chandelier. "I know the tale of Red Riding Hood even if I did not recognize it at the time. This was not the original Red. Our Red is lost, she has been since then. To everyone's horror, she'd been replaced by this little cloak girl."

My heart stopped.

Ice filled my veins.

Because I knew exactly who the Little Cloak Girl was.

Chapter Seven

"Whatever shall we do?"

— L. Frank Baum, The Wonderful Wizard of Oz

Without a shadow of doubt, I knew Scarlet was the same girl the Wizard of Oz confused as Dorothy. The palace walls shrunk around me. Not literally, but the squeeze in my chest and desire to run from Emerald City made the massive entryway feel as tight as the middle seat on an airplane.

I wanted more answers, more clues, and more clarity. I wanted to solve Storyland's first error, but I knew the one person who had experienced the error was the same person who had no idea what had caused the two worlds to collide. Even if Scarlet had been there in the very beginning of the blurring between Storyland and the human world, she was neither old enough nor aware enough to understand the details of the alternate universes.

"So," Kai started, still speaking to the wizard, "if you believe this girl was sent from the human world and the great and powerful Author erased the original Red, then why do you blame yourself for the story errors?"

Leave it to my husband, the history professor, to dig for details. He forced me to slow down and consider situations from every angle before acting on impulse—when I felt like it, anyway. Sometimes I simply could not wait. Even now, the urge to abandon Emerald City and run into the forest to hunt for clues overwhelmed me. I found my foot tapping and eyes shifting for the door or searching for a window through which I could spy the forest's tall trees in the distance. But only green glassy surfaces and reflected light surrounded us.

The Wizard of Oz frowned, looking ever more the sad old man that he'd become. "Because I was the one who sent the girl in the wrong direction. If only I hadn't meddled with her, perhaps she'd have found her story and all would be right with the world. One tiny mistake and it was like a ripple on the water, spreading and spreading until it finally ripped open the hole you call the rift where the story's magic leaks out. It is all connected which further proved Sherlock Holmes's theory of the singular Author."

"Hmm." Kai nodded, pursing his lips. "We call that spreading the Butterfly Effect." His gaze slid to me and his eyebrows lifted with a dash of hope. "What if we find the first error the Little Cloak Girl made in Red Riding Hood's story and we fix it?"

"Without Scarlet? The Little Cloak Girl is a little busy babysitting *our* girl…and boy." I said as I tilted my head side to side.

"That's what I'm saying. With Scarlet. We go back to Scarlet and jog her memory until we figure out what she knows about the 'Author' adding her into Storyland. I remember the details, Mari. *The Little Cloak Girl* was a legend that spanned centuries and was never traced back to an original storyteller or event in history. None of the historians have found the source the way they have with *Snow White* and Margaretha Von Waldeck. Or like *Hansel and Gretel*." He paused as color drained from his face. He swallowed hard, likely holding back the sickness caused by the *Hansel and Gretel* trigger. "That fairy tale was traced back to cannibalism in the Great Famine of the early thirteen-hundreds. If we know the inspiration behind *The Little Cloak Girl*, maybe we can piece together enough of the plot to separate it from *Little Red Riding Hood* and undo the mixing of stories. We can have

Scarlet come here and reverse the decisions she made as the Little Cloak Girl in Red's story, whatever those were. If we take the Little Cloak Girl out of the story where she replaced the protagonist, the real Red might return, putting everyone back into place."

I closed the small distance between us and gave his arm a squeeze. If he could lead me through Storyland's battleground with a few words of encouragement and a steady hand, I could offer him the same comfort. Even while my mind raced and body ached to get to Scarlet and jog her memory ASAP. I forced myself to stay in place and absorb the details.

"I'm listening," I assured him. "And you're right."

If we wanted to seal the rift and prevent the crossover from ever occurring again, we needed to go to the source, to the very beginning. It was up to us to trace the steps Scarlet took as the Little Cloak Girl. And to find those steps we needed to identify the author or the inspiration behind the original tale.

Every puzzle has pieces, every investigation clues, every story an inspiration.

"All we have to do is learn the history," I muttered, loud enough for only my husband to hear. Hope sparkled in his eyes and all triggered fear from his time as Hansel was wiped away.

"And rewrite it," he said.

"If only it were that easy."

We'd have to retake the steps. Or guide Scarlet to walk the path until she found her way out of *Red Riding Hood*. Would Storyland demand Scarlet stay with her story? *No. She came from the human world.* Once we separated the stories, I hoped Storyland would no longer claim her. *The Little Cloak Girl* was never a full story, never finished, never written with a real ending—only with the girl wandering the woods endlessly. Maybe if she took those unfinished steps, the end would take her back to our world and Red would return.

In a fog of hope and eager to get on with this investigation, I floated to the exit. Kai followed close behind and we'd all but forgotten the bald man and his palace.

"Good luck," the wizard called after us.

I glanced over my shoulder to see the poor man wringing his hands. Worry lined every wrinkle on his sagging face. He'd existed for an indeterminate amount of time with the regret and stress of having destroyed Storyland—at least based on his limited beliefs. Pity twisted my gut for the odd character. He'd helped us by sharing his knowledge and I wanted to return the favor.

I'll help him when I fix this. Stay focused, Mari.

I forged ahead, putting one foot in front of the other with a mixture of impatience egging me forward and the desire to help the wizard slowing my steps. It was an odd sensation, as if a war raged on within me. Two sides battled, one telling me to run ahead and the other begging me to fix what I could in the here and now.

At the doorway, between the splintered wood, I paused. "Thank you," I said to the Wizard of Oz, "for everything."

He gave me a curt nod of acknowledgment, and his throat bobbed in a serious swallow. I wanted to repay him with something small. Perhaps I could draw his enemy away from the palace.

My brow knitted, and I pointed at the broken board. "Hey, quick question. What is your beef with Oberon?"

Confusion flickered with the twitch of his cheek until I reframed the question. He squinted at the wooden sign tacked to his door and sighed. "Ah. The king of the fairies believes I have the magic to help him bring his wife back from the human world."

Oof. The memory of the woman interviewed on TV came rushing back. The innocent human had been struck with Titania's story aura. Or was she the real queen of the fairies?

"She went into the human world?" I repeated. "As in crossed through the rift and completely left Storyland?"

He nodded. "Puck, Oberon's servant rubbed a potion in her eyes to make her fall in love with a donkey. But she was close to the hole at the time and saw a human man on the other side. She fell in love with him and left Storyland and Oberon to be with him. Oberon believes I can help get her back since he doesn't know I'm not a real wizard. I-I've tried to tell him but he doesn't listen."

So the woman from the news story *was* the real Titania.

"Maybe Oberon will listen to me since I'm from the human world. I can tell him to leave you alone and that I'll help bring Titania back."

A sudden, overwhelming relief transformed the Wizard of Oz's face to a beaming grin. The short man stood taller as the weight lifted from his shoulders. "Well, good luck to you! Good luck in all of your endeavors. I cannot thank you enough for fixing my mistake."

"It isn't your mistake," I said. "Nobody but The Author's anyway."

Was I really buying into the all-powerful, god-like author notion? Had one person really written all of history's fairy tales? If that were the case, identifying *The Little Cloak Girl*'s creator would be a heck of a lot easier. All we had to do was identify the author of any story and we'd have our answer. Unfortunately, nothing was that easy. The writer was likely a proverbial needle in the haystack of history.

For now, the Wizard of Oz's relief was enough to satiate my need to help. Now all I wanted was a magical pair of red slippers. With two heel clicks I could teleport back to the human world without having to cross through a war country.

I swallowed the dread and let my excitement win me over. Excitement about the investigation ahead was the only way I'd survive another trip through Storyland.

I stepped outside, the first step of our journey home.

With Kai's hand in mine, we stayed the course along the yellow brick road. The painfully bright path kept my gaze focused on the immediate steps in front of me. One at a time, I forged on, ignoring the clash of King Arthur's sword against Queen Guinevere's stone body. Out of the corner of my eye, I caught sight of Medusa turning other characters from Camelot into stone. One by one, the gorgon's cursed gaze bested the Knights of the Round Table.

I hurried ahead, mumbling what Kai had told me earlier.

"I'll save them when I fix the rift. I'll save them when we fix this error."

Finally, I did the worst thing I could do. I looked back. The field of frozen characters gutted me and I found myself unable to move. Unlike them, I still had soft flesh and was free of Medusa's stare. It was my desire to save the day that had me standing stone still like a statue.

"Mari," Kai said. His voice was distant as if he spoke from the other side of a long tunnel. I tried to pull my attention from the field but I couldn't stop staring as Lancelot wept over Guinevere's stone body. King Arthur raised his sword to kill the knight who'd had an affair with his wife. This wasn't how the legend was supposed to go. King Arthur never killed Lancelot... but here I stood witnessing the beheading of the famous fictional knight. He swung the sword into the back of Lancelot's neck where it cut through skin and bone. Detached now, Lancelot's head fell against the queen's stony stomach with a sickening thud.

Kai's voice was a wobble of underwater words. I couldn't stop staring at the train wreck—the horror that had descended upon Storyland. With my eyes glued to the disturbing scene, I replayed one comforting thought. *I can fix this.*

Try as King Arthur might, he couldn't wake his wife with the thwack of his sword against the lifeless woman's rock-hard body.

Bile rose in my throat, and I ripped my hand free from Kai's hold. I doubled over, hands on my knees and let my vomit color the yellow brick road brown. The coffee I'd downed in the human world came up bitter.

I wiped my mouth and allowed my husband to tug me along. My gut swirled with dread every time my gaze strayed from the road in front of us. Just when I finally had the resolve to keep my eyes ahead, a prickling feeling crawled up the back of my neck.

Someone was watching me.

If I turned, would I meet Medusa's deadly gaze? A branch cracked behind us and my head snapped toward the sound. I hadn't realized we were passing through a forest. Tall trees lined both sides of the brick road, shadowing the pathway. The thick cover overhead made the forest as dark as night.

Two yellow eyes peered back at me.

The stalker's gaze crawled over my skin, pricking goosebumps over every bare surface. I pulled my sleeves over my hands and lifted my shoulders to sink my neck into the collar of my coat.

In a blink, the eyes vanished, and we emerged from the forest. The journey continued as uneventful as was possible for the chaos of Story-land. I wanted to shake away thoughts of the stalker in the forest but questions plagued me. Was it the wolf? Did he know we were on a quest to fix his story?

Though the forest was now on the horizon long behind us—or so it seemed—I felt eyes on me. I saw the shadow of a creature moving between the little Georgian houses in Jane Austen's English country-side. I heard the fall of their footsteps thudding in our wake.

Maybe a character wanted my help. It was wishful thinking, but so far the people of Storyland had not approached us. All I had to do was ignore them, too.

At the sight of the rift's jagged, paper edge, air filled my lungs. I'd been taking shallow breaths, only taking in enough air to stave off fainting. We picked up the pace, almost breaking into a run for home.

The foot falls behind us grew louder and caught our attention at the same time. We glanced over our shoulders but before I could make sense of the situation; the figure was upon us thrusting their arms out. Shimmering liquid splashed from the tiny bottle in the figure's fist, aimed directly at my husband. Kai yelped and slapped his hands to his eyes while I reached for the handle of my 9mm.

As the figure turned to me, uncapping another bottle, I tugged my gun from the holster and aimed it at the attacker. Too late. The liquid splashed into my eyes with a burn so shocking I dropped the weapon. The pistol clattered to the ground at the attacker's feet. Moments before the liquid blinded me I caught sight of the figure, identifying them as a wiry man with pointed ears and two protruding horns from his forehead.

The liquid only stung for a second more before my vision went red.

Chapter Eight

"My soul is in the sky."

— William Shakespeare, A Midsummer Night's
Dream

P anic squeezed my throat so tightly I couldn't scream or cry out for Kai. It didn't matter how many times I blinked or scratched at my eyes, I couldn't see. The elf-like attacker had blinded me with a liquid that turned my vision a rosy red.

Calm, Mari. Think. You've dealt with worse.

I slowed the thunderous beats inside my chest by elongating the exhale of each breath I took. After a few lungfuls, I found my voice.

"Kai, are you okay?" I asked.

Breathless, he said, "I can't see, but otherwise peachy. Wait—" A hand landed on my shoulder and my muscles jolted. Kai gave my bicep a reassuring squeeze. "I never noticed how sexy your neck is."

He never *what*? *What a random thing to say.*

"What the hell?" Before I could ask if his vision had returned, he spoke again and released his hold on me.

"I mean I've noticed, but now I've *noticed*!"

I fumbled around to find him, feeling for his arm or chest or anything to orient me. "Kai. Focus. We just got attacked by some wild —Oh!" The rosy curtain covering my eyes gradually faded. The world filled in around us, looking as it had before but with a tint of magenta. My husband shuffled closer to me, staring at me with his mouth hanging open. Like a puppy, he nearly drooled on my feet but I didn't mind. Why didn't I mind? Weren't we just in some kind of danger? I couldn't recall what had occurred right before Kai complimented me and I no longer cared because the man in front of me took all of my attention.

I never thought my Golden Retriever husband could be any cuter. Apparently I'd been wrong.

"Mari, you're radiant," he said. He slipped his arm around me and pulled me into him. "Have I ever told you that before? I should have told you that before. I need to tell you that more. You're radiant and I think we should dance." With a wiggle of his eyebrows, he embraced me with his other arm, pressing his front against me as he swayed side-to-side.

I melted into his hold until a distant rumbling ruined the moment. I blinked and tilted my head back, squinting at the storm clouds that darkened the world. Even the heavy gray clouds were lined pink at the edges. Droplets of water fell lazily, each rimmed with a sheen of rose. As much as I wanted to return my gaze to the handsome man before me, the storm nagged at me. In a few moments we'd be soaked, dancing in the rain in—where were we?

My gaze fell to the world around us. Over my lover's shoulder, a massive mushroom stood like a spongy tree in the distance. Or was it close enough to touch? I wiggled from my dance partner's hold and tried to reach for the springy mushroom but he caught my hand and spun me around, sweeping me up with twirling footwork.

From this angle, I spied a pile of rubble topped with a few gumdrops and draped in cracked white icing. I frowned at the odd candy-like house and shifted my attention to the unnaturally bright brick beneath our dancing feet. The yellow road spurred my memory. The Wizard of Oz. The Gingerbread Man. Wonderland.

"Storyland," I breathed, finally identifying our surroundings. "The mission. The—the—" I pulled away from Kai and spun to face the jagged crack in the middle of the world. The paper edges had torn open to reveal a swirling world beyond. Past layers of manuscript pages, I saw dull concrete and the base of a gray lamp post.

"My love," Kai said, his breath warm and inviting against my neck as he stepped up behind me and snaked his arms around my waist.

The admiration in his voice drew my attention, and I twisted, my gazing sliding to his face. Once I met his eyes, I couldn't look away. "Were we dancing?"

He grinned, and I sank into him, weak at the knees. "Dancing in the rain, Baby."

The rain? Another rumble of thunder rippled through the world and alarm bells went off in my head. *No. Dancing in a storm—in Storyland!* I couldn't fall into the spell again. "What were we doing before we started dancing?" What in the Wonderland had happened to my husband? To me? Memory of the elf-man returned. "Was that cupid who attacked us?" I strained to see around his head but Kai moved with me and tried to keep my gaze locked on him. "Kai." I struggled to pull from his embrace and failed. My husband was entranced, spellbound, hypnotized and so was I. I avoided his gaze, knowing I'd melt into his amorous eyes. A lightning bolt of agony shot through my skull. This dancing and the sudden love obsession was a trick from a potion—"It was Puck." How did I know our attacker had been the fairy character from Shakespeare's *A Midsummer Night's Dream*? Where did the information come from? Now was the time to be grateful for the sudden answers, not question the source.

"Mari…" Kai said breathlessly as he cupped my jaw with one hand and brushed his lips against my neck. "Mari, you're all I've ever wanted."

"Kai, stop!" *I mean, don't stop but*—"Stop!" He obliged, pulling back with a hurt look that knitted his brows. I tore my gaze from his before the spell swept me away again. "The potion won't work on me." All I had to do was not look at my husband and focus on the rift. I stared past him at the edge of the pages fluttering in the storm's wind. The pink rim was gone.

I blinked and scanned our surroundings to test my vision. Nothing was shaded with the rose-colored spell. The pink had vanished.

Kai reached up and tucked a strand of hair behind my ear. I caught his wrist in my grasp and dared to look at him. "Kai, listen to me."

He smiled goofily and his gaze fell to my lips.

Before he could try to kiss me, I patted his cheek—maybe with a little too much force. "Just look away from me."

He didn't listen. He didn't mind my little love slaps either. He simply leaned forward, puckering his lips for the kiss of the century, and one that'd probably last a century if I didn't nip this in the bud.

I grabbed his chin and yanked his head to look at the rift on our right. "Look," I said. "Look at where we are."

Kai blinked at it for a moment before turning to me. He cupped my jaw with both hands now and tugged my face toward his.

"It didn't work," I muttered before he drowned me in a breathless kiss. It was eager and wanting and incredibly sexy but now wasn't the time. I pushed him off of me with the heels of my hands against his breastbone. He stumbled back but never broke his gaze on my mouth. "Why didn't it work?" I nearly shouted now.

"Mari, I'm so utterly in love with you."

"I know," I said, patting his shoulder as I slipped away from another attempted hug. "I know you do. But I'm trying to save the world right now. We both are. Do you remember that? Do you remember when a fairy attacked us? Oberon's servant from the fairy realm in Shakespeare's play."

Kai shook his head and maintained a lopsided grin. "It's like you're breathing poetry to me."

It was no use. Kai was still under the spell that I'd broken free from. *Why didn't it work?* I searched the ground as if it had the answers but found my gun instead. Fat raindrops splashed against the brick road and shined against the surface of the pistol's black metal.

"Wherefore didn't t w'rk?" A voice echoed my thoughts, and I dropped into a crouch to snatch the weapon.

Slowly, I straightened, gun in hand, and turned on my heels. I grimaced at the horned fairy before me who looked neither interested nor threatened by the deadly barrel pointed square at his chest.

Instead, Puck stood with limp arms and hopelessness twisting his face. His jaw hung open, and his brow quirked as he eyed me. "Thou art free."

"From the love spell," I said. This frail fairy wasn't a danger—at least not now that his potion bottles were empty. My arms dropped, and I tucked the gun back into the holster, tugging my shirt and sweater over it. "Yeah. Apparently your little tricks don't work on me." I stepped closer and Puck matched my movement. He backed away with every step I took. I pinned him with a finger against his sternum. "Can you fix my husband?"

"I cannot."

I believed him. In the story, Puck screws up a lot, wreaking havoc across *A Midsummer Night's Dream* when he uses the potion to make the wrong characters fall in love. "All right, fine. So you're a failure. You probably thought he was Demetrius, and I was Helena. Right?" I threw the names of the characters around as if I'd read the play just this morning. Hell, I knew it so well I could have sworn I wrote the dang thing. The knowledge was convenient, but the migraine that came with it? Not so much.

Puck's eyes grew to the size of a golf ball. "Nay, that gent is the sir who hast stolen Titania's affection. At Oberon's hest, I has't thwart'd Titania's lov'r."

A laugh escaped me. Another one bubbled to the surface as I threaded the situation together, weaving the errors in a hideous pattern. "Let me get this straight. You think Kai is the human man Titania fell for." I pointed to my love-struck husband. "Now you're trying to fix it with another love potion? Got it." I snapped my fingers and smiled a joyless smile. "Great. This is awesome."

"I am fain thou art pleased."

Another laugh. Another mistake. Puck was truly a mess, but it wasn't his fault. Shakespeare wrote him as a meddling fairy of misadventure.

"Did you use less potion on me?" I asked, still scraping for answers.

Puck shook his head. "The potion ceased w'rking at which hour thou toldest t so."

Despite the fairy's Shakespearian way of speaking, I understood his meaning. Translating it for myself, I repeated his words and worked through the confusing situation with the facts. "I said it would stop working, so it stopped working."

As soon as I turned to Kai, his lips spread into a grin so wide it looked like his mouth would stretch off of his face. "Kai. Can you tell the potion to stop working?"

He didn't seem to hear me. Even when repeated, the question had no influence over my husband's behavior.

Back to square one.

After several more tries, I gave up. The magic only worked for me, apparently.

The rain poured steadily now, soaking the three of us. Puck stared at me. Kai stared at me. I stared at the rift. If we crossed over, would that break the spell on Kai? Did we have enough time to deal with this subplot drama before more hell broke loose and we found ourselves trapped in a never-ending cycle of Storyland errors? If I crossed over and grabbed Scarlet, would we figure out the history behind *The Little Cloak Girl* without Kai's help? Not likely. Scarlet had existed for hundreds of years as a Keeper of Stories. She hadn't even known she was the Cloak Girl until Kai had studied it. We needed the historical details to find the story and identify the plot.

A chill from the storm sank to my bones. The uncontrollable shivering that came with it jarred my focus on the situation.

I groaned as my shoulders fell. "I wish the storm would stop."

All at once the world brightened. I spun away from the rift and threw my head back, beaming up at the heavens. The clouds vanished as if Storyland's sky was a photo on a computer screen and my wish was the editing software that deleted the storm. I laughed—this time with joy and a hint of hope behind it.

"Thank you, Storyland!" I shouted at the sky. At least now I'd be able to think clearly.

I dropped my head, ready to forge ahead. Spell or no spell. I smiled at Puck but he was no longer looking at me. He raised his eyebrows as his gaze trailed past me, and my heart skipped as I followed his line of sight to the rift.

To my relief, the rift was unchanged. The layered manuscript was still torn just enough for me to see through to the other side but now three women stood between me and my escape.

Pride and Prejudice's Elizabeth Bennet, *Romeo and Juliet's* Juliet, and Jane Eyre shared matching expressions. They were the picture of old-fashioned romantic heroines with long, layered dresses that brushed the yellow brick road with thick hems. Each lady clasped her hands to her chest and smiled dreamily at me. Their eyes shifted to Kai who slid up to me and hooked an arm around my neck.

"You must allow me to tell you how ardently I want to get into your pants," he said.

"Oh, good grief," I said. I rolled my eyes at the ridiculous butchering of Mr. Darcy's famous pick up line. Even misquoted, the words had the same effect on the three ladies. They oohed and ahhed and clutched a handkerchief to their breasts. It was the picture of a love-sick swoon.

The most sensible of the characters—Elizabeth—stepped forward and said, "While I am a more rational creature than that of a woman begging for love, I wish for my story to be as it once was. You must not leave until you have taught us how to secure a man as you have. For it is a truth universally acknowledged—"

I raised my hand. "Let me stop you right there. I know the quote." Another jolt of pain shot through my temples and I almost claimed that I was the one who'd written the first sentence of Jane Austen's *Pride and Prejudice*.

I shook it off and ducked away from Kai's hold. The moment I freed myself, the three women crowded me. My heart thumped as I realized they were coming close to grab me like I was their prisoner.

I grunted and twisted my arm to reach for the weapon beneath my sweater but Juliet and Jane gripped me by the arms with unusual strength.

"You must not leave," Elizabeth repeated.

"I must not leave," I said with a sigh. Though I had impressive muscles from carrying the heaviest four-month-old in existence, I couldn't wriggle from the ladies's grasp. If I twisted my arm any more to reach for the gun, it might snap off.

As desperately as I'd tried to avoid fixing the stories during our journey, the stories had still found me.

And trapped me.

Chapter Nine

"O, teach me how you look, and with what art You sway the motion of Demetrius' heart."

— William Shakespeare, A Midsummer Night's Dream

Never could I have guessed that romance novels would be the most dangerous of all. At least that was how it felt based on the strength of Jane Eyre's grip on my arm and Juliet's hold on the other side. Their fingernails dug into the soft flesh just above my elbow as they *guided* me along in Elizabeth Bennet's wake.

The clank of swords and distant gunshots echoed through the atmosphere. Cannons boomed from somewhere on a sea I could not see. My skin prickled with the sensation of another stalker, someone watching us as they pulled me through the dark forest. But the faint growling in our wake was nothing compared to the sounds of death and destruction that consumed Storyland. The war raged with characters in constant battle. An occasional, disturbing scream split through the white noise of conflict and I wondered if Mother Goose had murdered Thumbelina or maybe the Cheshire Cat bit Goldilocks.

Jane and Juliet forced me forward, toward the Georgian houses in an English village. I had no choice but to fix their stories as quickly as possible and pray that they'd release me into the wild once they achieved their happily ever after—except for Juliet, of course. Though I supposed her version of happiness was sacrifice for the one she loved.

Our odd crew of three women in want of a man, a man in want of a woman, a fairy, and their hostage—AKA me—traveled deeper into Storyland. Though the journey only took moments, it felt like we'd walked miles. I twisted to glimpse the rift beyond the forest before they dragged me through the front doors of Longbourn estate. The Bennet family home was grand compared to the little apartments I was used to in San Francisco. Of course to the object of Elizabeth's reluctant affection, the estate was dismal.

She led us down a hall and into a quiet sitting room with a large mantle, a tea table, and plenty of plush sofas. Jane and Juliet yanked me down with them as they took a seat on a couch opposite Elizabeth.

Puck dawdled at the threshold of the room and Kai draped himself over the edge of the couch as he absently took a seat on the floor. The entire scene was as absurd as it was annoying. The women's fingers dug into my skin, nearly drawing blood as they beamed at my lovestruck husband. The useless Shakespearian fairy did nothing to help the situation. Instead, Puck kept his distance from the determined women, possibly afraid he'd mistakenly make one of them fall for Oberon or himself.

The more I wiggled away from the women, the tighter they held on and the more blood beaded to the surface. Red stained the flesh beneath their fingernails as I seethed and sucked air through gritted teeth.

"If I help, will you let me go?" I asked, keeping my jaw clenched.

Elizabeth clasped her hands in her lap and nodded primly. "I have but one question for you. How did you see past your gentleman's faults?"

"I—wait," I paused. Were the romances unaffected by Storyland's errors? Elizabeth was infamous for her judgment of Mr. Darcy. According to the original novel, she represented the prejudiced half of the novel's title. With a question surrounding Mr. Darcy's faults, it seemed *Pride and Prejudice* wasn't disrupted. "Are you in love with Mr. Darcy?"

Elizabeth's mouth twitched, but she did not answer.

I ignored the dull pain in my arms and twisted to Jane Eyre. "Have you fallen for Mr. Rochester?"

Jane's eyelids slid over her big green eyes in a slow blink. "I have." Sadness swam in her unseeing gaze. "But he has not. He…" her faint voice faded, and a hiccup interrupted her momentary silence. "Just as Romeo, Mr. Rochester admires the Queen of Hearts and has taken residence in Wonderland."

I bit back a sudden laugh. *Of course these romance heroes fell for Alice's antagonist.* Of course the answer was more insane than my wildest dreams. I prayed the fix was as simple as reminding the characters of their plot.

"Tell me," Juliet said, "how can I convince mine own family to alloweth me to love Romeo? As thee has't with him?" She pointed at Kai with her free hand.

I scraped my brain for memory of Shakespeare's tragic romance until the details came back in a rush, bringing with them a headache. I'd studied the play once in high school, but I remembered every line as if I'd memorized each word only yesterday. Unlike Elizabeth, Juliet was confused about her story. She'd never convince House Capulet to accept the Montagues because it wasn't the way of the plot.

"I didn't," I said, turning to Juliet. I winced as she gripped tighter and a little gasp escaped her. "I didn't convince my family to let me be with my husband. And you won't either. Your family and Romeo's family hate one another and you will not change that. You *shouldn't* change that." It was a risk to tell her the tragic truth with the way her fingers buried into my flesh, but I had no other choice. Fixing the fairy tales and stories had always come with a price and that was what I came here to do.

I held Juliet's gaze, her sienna eyes growing sadder by the second.

"I'm sorry it was written this way," I said, a pang of guilt twisted in my gut, shoving bile up my throat. The acidic vomit tasted bitter at the back of my tongue. Where did this shame come from? I wasn't Shakespeare. Though I hadn't decided innocent Juliet's fate, the guilt was as palpable as if I'd wielded the ink in my own hands and created this tragic ending. "Don't shoot the messenger." I breathed in a small voice. "But yours is a love that has served as a warning to readers throughout history, and that should not change." Since when had I become a literary analyst? The words flowed as easily as if I'd prepared the speech, or pulled them directly from 'mine own' heart. "The story of you and Romeo teaches that tragedy results from pure love in an imperfect world. It creates awareness that personal conflict affects innocent people around us, including the next generation, and that miscommunication can kill."

A distant, shrill cry broke the silence as Storyland's war claimed another victim.

Despite the tears welling in Juliet's warm eyes, she nodded. She understood. Finally, she released her hold on my arm and relief flooded me. Though the crescent wounds left by her fingernails throbbed with a dull ache, I could breathe again.

Juliet shot to her feet as tears streamed down her cheeks. "I wilt kill the Queen of Hearts so we can die by our family's feud!"

"What?" That certainly wasn't the right ending! I shook my head. "No, no."

Her brows knitted together as she looked down at me.

"Well, I guess it's not entirely wrong," I mumbled. "Yes, your story must end with you and Romeo in love and in death."

"I wilt do as you bid," she said. The honesty in her eyes stopped me. Juliet was willing to sacrifice whatever former plan she'd had to win over Romeo for what I wanted, and I was merely a stranger in a strange land. *So why does she care for my instruction?* Should I even question it, or should I accept this miraculous blessing?

"Anything I bid?" I asked, testing the waters. I scanned the women's faces as they nodded. They listened intently, eager for my next instruction. If I could get Jane to release my arm, would they let me walk out of here? I turned to Charlotte Bronte's heroine and narrowed my eyes. "Jane, what if I told you that letting go of me will make Mr. Rochester see how gentle you are?"

"Will it?" Jane asked.

"Try it," I said. "Let go."

Jane released me. More air rushed into my lungs. The cuts on the side she'd gripped weren't as deep as Juliet's, but they still stung when air hit the open wound. I swallowed a groan and focused on the positive, Jane had heard me.

"Jane, stand up and escort Juliet to the tea table," I said.

She did. My spirits lifted slightly as hope rose on the horizon. I was free, and they were listening. Juliet graciously accepted the escort with her arm hooked through Janes. While they walked, they kept their gazes fixed on me in a creepy, head-swiveling and neck-twisting way.

The women did not blink, perhaps fearing I would run, and they'd lose their guide. Sure, Kai and I had a great marriage, and he appeared to be grossly head-over-heels in love with me thanks to Puck's idiocy, but I wasn't a romantic genius. Still, the heroines waited for me to speak as if I was the boss of their lives.

Could I fix their stories with nothing more than a few suggestions? Did these women believe in me enough to do anything I said? Better to test the theory as soon as possible and get the heck out of here.

"Elizabeth," I said, turning my attention to the most stubborn of the characters. If I had her in the palm of my hand, surely the other two love-struck ladies would listen. But the request would have to be as absurd as the situation in order to push the boundaries and give my theory a true test. I glanced around the room for ideas of a chaotic demand. "Kiss him." I twisted to point at Puck in the doorway.

The fairy spun and tried to run but Elizabeth was on him as if she'd teleported across the room. As soon as the words came out of my mouth, the heroine's mouth was on his and shock rippled through me. Adrenaline pumped through my veins with a newfound energy and I stood, resisting the urge to cover the stinging wounds with my palms.

When Elizabeth released him, Puck darted out of sight.

"Wait!" I shouted. "Come back."

Puck obeyed, appearing in front of me in a blink. To my absolute delight, the fairy believed in me as much as the romance heroines did. Because of this belief, I held an unexplainable power over his actions. I accepted the oddity because it was time to roll with the positives and use everything that worked to my advantage.

"When you return to Oberon, tell your fairy king to leave the Wizard of Oz alone," I said.

He nodded and backed away in a slight bow. "Yes."

"And fix my husband!" I pointed at Kai on the floor. Puck nearly tripped over Kai's legs as he scooted away from me.

The fairy grimaced, his expression growing gaunt. "Mine own mistress, only thee has't the power now. F'rgive mine own mistake."

With that, he fled, giving Elizabeth a wide berth as he passed her. Was Puck right? Did I have the power to fix Kai? I'd attempted to rid him of the potion by asking him to tell it off before. If anybody believed in me, it was Kai. The same strange magic that I held over the women and our funny little fairy friend should be easily wielded in Kai's case.

I slid to the floor and knelt beside my husband, taking his hands in mine. "Kai. Tell the potion it does not have power over you."

When he repeated my words, the fog lifted from his gaze. He found my eyes and gave me a funny smile that warmed me from the inside out. This was the look of genuine affection I knew and loved, not obsession brought on by a trickster's potion. "That was some potent love juice," he said.

"You're back?"

Shaggy hair bobbed as he nodded and confirmed my suspicions with a full grin. "I'm back, Baby."

I squeezed his hands before standing and turning my demands to the women in the room. "Jane and Juliet, go together to Wonderland. Ignore the Queen of Hearts and retrieve your gentlemen. Tell them Mari demands that they love you with all of their hearts."

Juliet smiled, and Jane nodded. The pair vanished and after a moment, the white noise of war fell quieter. Cries and clanking swords didn't disappear entirely, but the tension in the air eased ever-so-slightly.

It worked.

Even in the bowels of fairy tale hell, I'd found an escape from the women who'd held me hostage. Only Elizabeth remained holding a frown of confusion over her quivering chin—quivering with anger it seemed. I cringed. Before she could lecture me, or judge me, I told her what to do next based on the original plot. I told her to overcome her prejudice in order to complete her character arc. "Find Mr. Darcy and when he proposes to you again, accept."

Like the others, she vanished.

Free now, all Kai and I had to do was survive another quick trip through Storyland. Through Storyland *and* through the dark forest.

Just survive.

Chapter Ten

"How shall we cross the river?"

— L. Frank Baum, The Wonderful Wizard of Oz

It turned out some idioms were accurate. Practice truly made perfect—or at least slightly better in this case. Even though the space changed, the woods extended longer and blocked the view I'd had of the rift before; I was ready for the journey. I'd survived Storyland once and vowed to do the same a second time despite the shifting landscape.

I would not stop to interfere with stories, and I would not look back. Not even when I heard the growling.

The low rumble followed our every step through the forest. Kai and I exchanged glances, but we did not look back. He positioned himself one step behind me, between my body and the base of the trees and shrubs that walled the road. I tugged my gun from the holster and carried it barrel down against my hip.

Déjà vu hit me like a book to the face. How many pages of this journey had we already suffered? How many stalkers and beasts would I have to face before I could finally breathe? Twice I'd faced the Big

Bad Wolf. Twice I'd followed the yellow brick road in an attempt to escape Storyland. Twice I'd wished to wear the hood again, if only to survive long enough to create a better world for my children—for all the children and innocent people in San Francisco and beyond.

I tried to picture the playground at Pioneer Park because as long as I maintained the image of a simple and sweet gathering place; I wasn't thinking of the wolf in the woods. I wasn't tempted to turn around and try to shoot him before he attacked us. There was no telling how much faster and more powerful he'd be in his own territory. My gun had barely worked on the half-human version of him when the story aura had taken over a San Francisco serial killer. It took gutting the wolf from the inside out to stop him—and that was on my turf, in a world where time didn't wobble and space held real measurements.

Shadows played tricks, casting long stretches of darkness that seemed unending. The only reprieve through the forest was the brick beneath my feet. Though I preferred the simplicity of San Francisco's gray concrete, the yellow road was as close as I could get. It felt *almost* entirely solid, grounding me in a world where common sense and logic held no value.

As the rough rumble grew louder, we picked up the pace. Kai grabbed my free hand and helped me to match his speed. For the second time that day—or week, or hour—we ran for the rift.

Shrouded in darkness, I couldn't see our escape just yet but I knew we simply had to follow the road. Follow the road and look forward. My pulse thundered to keep up with the burst of spent energy. If only I'd kept up with the yoga session, or actually showed up to more than one spin class, maybe Kai wouldn't have to drag me. He moved with a practiced runner's ease while I clunked along behind and gasped for air.

The growl built and built and built. My heart matched every rising rumble with a doubled beat. My heels hit the brick hard, sending jolts of pain into my calves.

"You can do it," Kai said. My struggle came in the quick breaths I grappled for while sweat dripped down my face and over my open mouth.

Never had I loved the color yellow so much. At the end of the forest, the darkness subsided, and the brick shimmered against the glow of the moon. Night had fallen while we traveled through the forest though surely more than a single day had passed. Or was it only a few minutes ago that we'd spoken with the Wizard of Oz? It didn't matter now because the rift was on the horizon.

I sucked oxygen through swollen airways and willed my legs to stop burning. It didn't work, but the distance was a mirage. What had looked a mile away, only took a few steps. In front of the rift now, Kai stepped through, keeping his grip tightly entwined with my fingers.

I followed with a firmly placed foot on the other side. Gray sidewalks that were scattered with smashed gum, dead leaves, and an occasional fast food wrapper came into view.

The faded colors of the play structure's slide and monkey bars was the most beautiful sight I'd seen since the birth of my children. Even the litter blowing in the breeze of the empty park passed as a warm welcome compared to the tornados and beheadings in Storyland.

Before I could lift my other leg, something snagged the bottom of my sweater and ripped me off my feet. A force more powerful than Jane and Juliet's unnatural strength yanked me back, leaving nothing but my outstretched arm in the human world. My spine slammed against the brick, and the wind knocked from my lungs. Despite the attack, I held fast to my husband's hand as my arm twisted up and behind me, pulling the joint from the socket in my shoulder. The ache of dislocation radiated from the joint and I cried out in pain.

A huff of hot air came out with a snarl and I recognized the sound immediately. *The wolf.*

Kai's frame filled the rift's crack as he wrapped his other hand around my wrist and pulled me toward him. I flipped to my knees but couldn't crawl any closer. The jaws on my sweater were twice as strong as the adrenaline pumping through my veins.

"Don't let go!" I screamed.

Terror gripped Kai as he tore his eyes from the wolf and focused on me. "I won't."

But the villain didn't give him a chance to keep his promise. The wolf yanked me away from the rift and from my husband's hold. One moment, I was begging Kai to hang on and the next I was on my back beneath a seven-foot beast.

The wolf's massive paws splayed out on either side of my head. Long claws scraped the brick, the sound grating and right next to my ears. With another growl, he bared his shining white fangs and foamy saliva dripped from the sharp tips of his canines like ice melting from stalactites. Fear choked me, squeezing my throat and pinning me to the ground.

He licked his lips with a long crimson tongue, and when he snarled, the hoarse sound molded around a recognizable word. "Red." He breathed.

Adrenaline finally gave me a boost of clarity. I still had my weapon. With my good arm, I aimed the barrel at the base of the wolf's ribcage. I flicked off the safety and pulled the trigger.

Silence.

Nothing happened.

I fired again, but no bullet was released. The gun didn't discharge though I was sure I'd properly tested and prepared it. I pulled the trigger again and again to no avail.

The wolf's enormous mouth spread into a disturbing grin of glistening teeth. "What are you doing out here, little girl and where are you going?" He said his line as it was written—as if I was Red Riding Hood. Again.

Sickness surged in my throat, and my stomach clenched. His attack on me didn't make sense since I no longer wore the hood and I didn't carry the story aura anymore. Of course, when I'd ended *Little Red Riding Hood,* it was in the human world…here in Storyland the tales reincarnated over and over and the real red was still missing.

And if confusion had made the Three Billy Goats Gruff attack Cinderella, surely the wolf could mistake me for the absent protagonist from *Little Red Riding Hood.*

I just needed to buy time until help came.

If I played along with the plot, maybe it'd give Kai an opportunity to help before the wolf devoured me. The theory gave me a dash of hope.

"I'm going to my grandma's house," I said as I slowly rolled to the side and tried to wiggle out from under him.

My theory fell flat when the wolf didn't respond by running off to find grandma's house. Instead, he swiped at me, slamming against my chest with his claws on my sternum. The shock of it rippled through my bones as the nodules of my spine made contact with the brick. He easily pinned me between his paw and the ground, giving me no room for escape. The pain in my dislocated shoulder left my vision temporarily blurred, and I wanted to give in to the darkness that beckoned.

Blackness crept in at the edges of my eyes and the spinning in my head threatened to pull me under. The shred of consciousness that kept me aware was more torture than it was helpful. If I fainted, I would no longer suffer, I'd be swallowed in peace and darkness for a final rest after years of chasing fairy tales. All I wanted was to rest…

Hot breath dampened my face. My eyes popped open and rows of jagged teeth spread over my head and then clamped until pressure from the tips bit into the crown of my skull. Adrenaline shot through my veins and I squeezed the gun. With renewed energy—however temporary—I gripped the weapon and swung at the wolf's temple with the base of the handle.

The wolf snapped back with a yelp, releasing me before his canines broke skin. I sucked in a breath and called out for my husband's help. When the sound of footsteps assured me Kai was right beside me, I twisted my neck to see feet coming closer. He ran right up to the wolf, near enough to brush the matted fur…until he passed us. It wasn't Kai at all.

I tipped my head back for an upside-down view of the newcomer.

"Hey!" I cried.

A woman in a dark dress—no, a witch—glanced down at me. The sight of her seemed to spark a sudden migraine that joined the pain already wracking my body. *Mother Gothel.* The villain from Rapunzel's story only responded with a wicked smile. Behind her, Kai was crossing through the rift but her Storyland strength easily shoved him back into the human world with a blast of sorceress magic. There was no other explanation for the hunched, frail old woman's ability to push a grown man aside. The witch peered into the human world as a grunt came from the other side and Kai hit the ground.

With skeletal fingers and a bony hand, Mother Gothel shakily grasped her skirts and then stepped through the rift.

"Help!" I begged in a last-ditch attempt to demand her aid. Either she didn't believe in me the way the other characters had or she didn't care. Coming from a villain, both were equally plausible.

Mother Gothel gave me one last look before abandoning me to my death.

The wolf's breath came in hot wet puffs against my face. Recovered from the whack, he grinned again and snaked his tongue out over his snout. His neck stooped and his fangs nearly brushed my cheek as his jaws opened.

I pulled the trigger on instinct but it clicked uselessly.

"Little girl, your tools do not work in my woods," he said, drawing his long tongue over his black lips. Saliva splashed from the lick and landed warm and sticky on the top of my ear. It dripped down through the curves and crevasses to the inside of my ear.

His jaws expanded wide enough to swallow my entire head. The black abyss inside shadowed me in darkness and I squeezed my eyes shut. I had no weapon and no way of escape. Tears filled my eyes and slipped through my tightly sealed lids. They dripped down the side of my face like little rivers of rushed memory.

After everything I fought for, I was still going to die as the wolf's dinner.

Chapter Eleven

"Were the world mine…"

— William Shakespeare, A Midsummer Night's
Dream

Saliva and tears pooled in my ears, and I muffled a cry. Was this my final sacrifice? I could only hope that when the wolf devoured me, the errors in Storyland would correct themselves and the rift would seal shut. I could only hope this sacrifice—the way *Little Red Riding Hood* was supposed to end—would save Wendy and Jack and all of San Francisco from the aura that stripped innocent people of their agency and demanded they become characters tied to tragic and inescapable fates.

Because of the pain, I could only hope it'd all be over soon. Darkness encompassed me and I lost all sense of the surrounding world except pure pain.

After a thud, the wolf yelped, and the pressure on my chest lifted. Relief lasted only a moment before he slammed a massive paw against my aching shoulder again. I tried to scream, but it came out as a pathetic groan and I twisted to protect the injured side. Why wasn't it over yet? *End it. Eat me.*

A familiar voice shouted my name, and I slipped from darkness into a sudden nightmare where I'd fallen into black waters. I was drowning and my husband called for me from the surface.

"Kai," I whispered. I stretched my arm to reach out of the water and beg for help but my fingers found warm, matted fur. I tightened my grip around the hard object in my hand, feeling the ridges of the cold metal against my fingers. "The gun…" It didn't work in Storyland.

I blinked the darkness away. The hulking beast turned its attention to Kai with a snarl. A rock smashed into the wolf's head but he barely flinched. It was enough. The attack gave me a moment to think clearly.

"Catch!" I screamed and arched my back and neck to find Kai. I used all of my strength to swing my good arm back and launch the gun behind me. It clattered and slid across the brick. The metal scraped over the rough surface with a clatter and landed within arm's reach of Kai. He crouched, snatched the gun, and then steadied to aim it between the wolf's eyes. When he pulled the trigger it clicked just as it had for me. "Outside," I said, my voice raspy. "Shoot from the other side of the rift!"

The low rumble of the wolf's growl built from his bowels and bubbled to the surface with a laugh. Yellow eyes looked down at me, his prey. He laughed until a bullet sunk into his right shoulder. The solid muscle spasmed and blood quickly soaked the surrounding fur, dark and shining. His head flicked up, and he snapped at the air with his jaws while the sticky blood dripped and splashed across my forehead, making my hairline slick with the warm liquid.

The gun fired again, this time embedding into the wolf's skull. Where his yellow eye had stared hungrily at me, only a hole remained, steaming with the heat of his bubbling blood. Kai had hit him directly in the head.

Still, two bullets wouldn't stop a starving wolf.

He fixed his hungry gaze on me, darting his eye to the sticky blood on my face. His single eye blinked. "Better to see you with, my dear."

No. The story wasn't done yet. Fear clutched my gut, but I forced it down and focused on the scrap of adrenaline left trickling through my veins. I tried to shove his jaws away from me by smacking the heel of my hand against his snout.

"Don't call me dear," I said through clenched teeth as I pushed his face only an inch.

His mouth split open again and then closed around two of my fingers with a snap. A scream erupted from deep within me as the bite pushed the boundaries of pain. My arm shook but shock kept it upright as I stared at my hand where two fingers were now completely missing.

The wolf flicked his tongue over his lips. "Better to eat you with my..." his line cut short as if his brain had short-circuited. His mouth hung open in silence and his one eye blinked in confusion. He expanded his jaws slightly, but no words came out with the breath that steamed in the air.

He couldn't find his voice or the words. He couldn't finish the sentence. Which meant...

Could I control him the way I'd controlled the Puck and the heroines? "Find Red." I breathed, not loud enough to reach his ears over the roar of another gunshot. The world swirled with colors as the agony of stinging injuries overloaded my senses. I forced a pathetic cough to clear my raspy throat. "Leave! Go to the woods and wait for Red Riding Hood."

All at once, the pressure from his paw, his hot breath, the warm blood dripping from his eye and shoulder stopped. The wolf launched over me and threw himself through the rift. Kai discharged another two shots but the scrape of claws against concrete told me the bullets didn't slow his hunt.

Just like the other characters, he'd listened to me—no, he'd *obeyed* me.

With the immediate threat gone, shock melted away, and the pain doubled with every second that passed. My shoulder, my fingers...

Blood poured from where they should have been. The bite left me without the last two fingers on my left hand and my wedding ring was gone, swirling somewhere deep within the belly of the beast.

Footsteps framed my head. Shock strung me along in a state of total awareness as Kai stooped and slipped his arms in the crook beneath my knees and my torso. Every sound, feeling, and color was heightened when he straightened with a grunt and lifted me off the brick. My head lolled back, my neck limp as pain sucked my energy elsewhere.

"You're alive, Mari," he said, his voice tight. "You're alive and you're going to stay that way." He panted as he stepped over the rift's edge and carried me across the threshold between worlds like a broken bride—a bride who'd lost her wedding ring and the finger on which to wear it all thanks to a relentless and reincarnating villain. "You're not a damn sacrifice." He'd said it more to himself than to me.

I let my eyelids slide shut and shroud me in a darkness that was finally comforting. It invited me to rest, but I wasn't ready to slip away into unconsciousness. The wolf was out there prowling somewhere in the human world. Would he confuse Wendy for Red? Or Scarlet? Would he devour another innocent girl or murder a woman on her walk through Pioneer Park as the story aura wolf had all those years ago?

I'd saved myself only to doom someone else.

"Take me to Reese," I said, my last request before the shadow of sleep claimed me. I needed bandaging and medical care, but I also needed to make a plan. The medical examiner and Hunchback of Notre Dame was my best bet because he knew of the story aura long before any of us. With him I could get medical care and work through the story aura issues and how the magic worked both in and outside the rift.

"We need to get you to the hospital."

"Kai, please." I begged.

He grunted an unintelligible response and started walking. Night had fallen, and the park was devoid of life other than the distant patter of a jogger's footsteps. Dim lamp posts offered a foggy glow over the pathway, keeping the tree cover from the darkness of Storyland's woods. Through slitted lids, I watched the trees pass by as Kai carried me from the park.

The world brightened when we emerged from the path and onto San Francisco's sidewalk where car headlights zipped by in flashing beams and checkered yellow dotted the windows of towering buildings. The city never slept, not entirely. Stark lights, honking traffic, and echoing sirens were a comfort. I soaked in the sounds of home. For a moment, anyway.

How long until the wolf went on a murderous rampage and the sirens' screeches multiplied?

"Hurry," I mumbled. Thankfully, the morgue was close and Reese lived in the building next door. Close or not, walking with my dead weight in his arms would take time.

"I'm trying," he said between breaths. Though the steady rhythm of his pace lulled me, I forced my eyes open to stay conscious for a conversation with Reese. Cheering and laughter drifted from a nearby bar and it helped to keep me awake. A car screeched by, flooring the gas pedal to speed through a yellowing stoplight and the red and blue flashes of a police vehicle followed. The scattered distractions kept my mind busy and pulled my attention from the growing pain. At least I could rely on good ol' San Francisco with its reckless drivers and raucous partiers to keep me conscious.

I wouldn't wish for my city to be any other way. People were free to make their own choices here, not caught in the infinite loop of reincarnated stories.

Images of Storyland's war flashed through my mind. Of Lancelot's lifeless head and of the dead mermaid at the base of Rapunzel's tower. Of the witch who'd escaped into our streets. Now that I didn't have a wolf trying to bite my face off, an epiphany dawned. Fluttering heartbeats joined my already-erratic pulse at the thought of Mother Gothel in San Francisco. If she stayed true to her story, she was here to hunt for Rapunzel.

And if I had any energy or anything in my stomach, I might have vomited.

"Kai," I said, not loud enough for him to hear. "She's coming to kidnap Scar's…" A cough interrupted me and it didn't matter because I couldn't put enough energy into my voice for him to understand me over the city's white noise. Along with the words, I faded as my eyelids sealed shut.

Chapter Twelve

"Though she be but little, she is fierce!"

— William Shakespeare, A Midsummer Night's
Dream

I woke to the sound of Reese's heavy footsteps. The medical examiner who had been claimed by the Hunchback of Notre Dame's story aura walked with a limp that became more pronounced each time I saw him. The unsteady gait, thump thumped, growing louder and closer.

My eyes peeled open only to be blinded by the white track lighting overhead. Like a corpse, I was on my back on the cold steel table where medical examiners dissected bodies to determine the cause of death. But I was alive. Barely.

Squinting, I made out the shapes of Kai and Reese's faces as they hovered over me. At least their heads blocked the light from completely blinding me. The wracking pain in my hand and shoulder had subsided to a dull thud that sharpened slightly with the pressure of my pulse. I groaned and raised my arm to see the thick white bandages that were wrapped around my entire left hand, leaving only the spared fingers free.

I swallowed and tried flexing my fingers. The attempt left my head spinning because I thought I'd felt my ring and small finger despite their absences. Nothing was beneath the bandage except wounds and yet I swore I was curling and expanding all five fingers. If I focused on the phantom limbs any longer, the spinning would swirl me straight back to dreamland.

The warmth of Kai's palm distracted me as he gently brushed the hair back from my forehead. I dropped my arm to the table and tilted my head to his touch. He stooped over me and gave my head a half hug by pressing his cold cheek to mine. Behind him an exit sign glowed red over a closed door and ceiling vents pumped chilly conditioned air into the room. Without rolling over, I knew the other side of the morgue was lined with refrigerated cabinets that stored dead bodies.

"You almost had me in the second half," he said, voice light but shaking. "I thought maybe the bite gave you an infection."

A rush of breath escaped my nose in a faint laugh and I let my eyes fall shut again. "Yeah? Did I pass out in your arms like a true damsel in distress?"

"You should have seen me carrying you like a knight in shining armor over the hill on Main Street."

I opened my eyes and met his gaze. "So the infection?"

Reese rapped his knuckles against the steel table causing me to twitch at the knocking sound. "No infection. And no fingers. I can't sew them back on for you after you feed them to a wolf, you know?"

I frowned. As if I'd offered my hand to a villain for a snack. At least I wasn't Snow White who was hunted for her organs to feed to an evil and jealous queen. *Way to look at the bright side, Mari. You're a champ.*

Really, there was no bright side other than our survival and the dismal clues we'd gathered from our conversation with the Wizard of Oz. I refreshed myself on the plan and pictured each step in my mind with the colors from an imaginary block of notecards.

I assigned blue for research on *The Little Cloak Girl*'s historical hints or details that might lead us to the original telling. If we knew the plot, Scarlet could take the steps to move away from *Red Riding Hood* and make room for the original character.

Next came yellow. The second most important order of business was warning Scarlet about Mother Gothel, the witch who wanted to steal the child in her womb.

And last, but most importantly, we had to find and kill the wolf before he went on a rampage through the city, eating anyone who he might mistake as Red. I'd been down that road before. I'd witnessed the murder and bloodshed in the park, in front of my house. The wolf chosen by the story aura had even killed my neighbor's adult daughter and left her body on my doorstep.

I would not let it happen again.

Or had it already begun? Hopefully, the wolf would stay focused and only hunt for me—for Red, but I couldn't be sure.

Despite the ache, I twisted toward Kai. "How much time passed?"

Kai raked his hand through his messy hair and sighed. "My estimate is that we were in Storyland for eight human days. Or earth days. Or whatever." He waved his hand in a rotating gesture.

"Longer than a week?" I squeaked. "Wendy must miss us—"

"I already called Scarlet," he said. "While Reese was sewing you up. Sorry but I couldn't watch. Your hand looked awful." He smiled sheepishly and shoved his hands into his pants pockets. "You know I've passed out watching you in pain before..." his voice faded as he referenced the time he fainted on the hospital floor when I'd given birth to our daughter. "So I went outside to get better service on my phone and called to check in. Wendy has been asking when we'll be back, of course, but they're both healthy. Carlos was the one who answered since Scarlet needs her pregnant beauty sleep and he was already awake holding Jack. He said they tried to stay the first night at their place but ended up at our house because it's easier for the kids."

"Good," I said. "But what I meant was, how long has it been since we lost sight of the wolf?"

He grimaced and glanced at the watch on his wrist. The electronic timepiece lit up with a shining screen. "Two hours?"

"Too long." I rolled onto my good shoulder.

"Oh, no you don't," Reese said as he grabbed my ankle before I could swing it over the side of the table. He pointed at my other shoulder. "We still have to set this."

My gaze flicked to the limp limb, and I groaned. "You couldn't have done that while I was unconscious?"

He shook his head. "What did you expect? I'm one man, not a full-service hospital. The blood gushing from your hand was priority number one. Now, lie back so I can lodge this arm back into place." He patted the table.

I shot Kai a cringing look and didn't move. "We came here because I wanted to go over the information we learned with you. But I wasn't thinking clearly because now I see we don't have time to sit around and chat. We need to track down the wolf before we deal with the rift."

With a sigh Reese adjusted his glasses and tapped my arm. "You aren't tracking any wolves until I fix this shoulder. So, let's get on with it."

Another groan escaped me. I couldn't help it after everything we'd just been through. The threat of more agony invited the return of nausea and dizziness.

"Listen," he continued, "I know you want this arm relocated so you can get out of here as quickly as possible. Lie back and give me your wrist." He flicked his fingers in a beckoning demand.

Apparently, the medical examiner I'd worked with over the years knew me better than I expected. Finally, I obeyed, and he gripped my wrist with icy fingers. The cold shot a pang of guilt through me. I'd missed eight days of my children's lives and we didn't have time to spare to snuggle them before we'd return to the streets. Once we hunted the wolf—however long that'd take—we'd have to leave them again for Storyland and I hated the thought of saying goodbye to Wendy at the rift a second time.

Reese straightened my arm out to a ninety-degree angle. He firmly steadied my wrist and then slowly pulled harder and harder and harder until biting my tongue no longer kept my gasp silent. The agony heightened as the joint shifted and finally—finally; the bone slid back into the socket with a clunk.

I drew a sharp breath of the morgue's cold air. The refreshing chill calmed me and the persistent throbbing eased into a lingering ache. Reese instructed me to sit up as he fastened a makeshift sling to support my arm. The cloth bandage balanced my elbow in a white hammock after he tied the top over my neck and shoulder.

"This will keep it in place while the joint heals," he said, and then he tilted his head to be sure I met his gaze. "Do not use your arm or it will disrupt the recovery."

I nodded.

"No." He used two fingers to point at his eyes and then turned them on me to indicate that he was watching me. "I'm serious about this, Mari. Let it heal before you go hunting magical beasts. I won't have you get eaten because you didn't listen."

Kai bobbed his head. "That's right. You tell her, Reese!" He thrust out a fist in an offer to bump it but the medical examiner only blinked at Kai's hand before he turned his attention to me again.

"Kai has told me about the reincarnation in Storyland," he said, adjusting his glasses higher on his crooked nose.

I shook my head. "There isn't time to go over it right now. Just like before, I bet the wolf will use nighttime to hunt, and we only have a few more hours of darkness to find and kill—"

Reese slammed the table beside my leg with an open palm. "No!"

I jumped, and the movement sent aches rippling throughout my muscles and joints.

He continued, his narrowed gaze sharp and determined. "You will heal first, Mari Rowan, because I refuse to let you walk out of here only to come back in a body bag. Do you hear me? I do not want to have to store you in there." He spun the swiveling chair to the side and pointed at the wall of refrigerated cabinets. "And heaven knows I don't have the emotional strength to support this guy in the event of your murder."

I followed his line of sight as Reese met Kai's gaze. They were teaming up against me, and as much as I wanted to ignore the warnings and run at the wolf headfirst, I knew they were right. I'd become the sacrifice I was trying to avoid, and with the new information about the Cloak Girl's interference and the beginning of Storyland's errors, it no longer seemed that feeding myself to the wolf was the right answer. I'd die in vain, hoping to fix the rift I thought I'd split open when I continued to thwart the fairy tales' original endings.

"Fine." I relented. "Then let's take this time to talk about what we've learned. You've existed as a fairy tale character longer than any of us." My mind drifted to the wolf's behavior when I'd told him not to call me 'dear' and then to the women and Puck who'd instantly obeyed my demands. "Did you ever feel compelled—like forced—to do exactly what Scarlet asked of you when she was The Keeper of Stories?"

Reese blinked rapidly and then reached up to pluck his glasses off of his nose. He rubbed at his eyes and returned the glasses where they'd left little indents in his flesh. "Scarlet has always been a very convincing individual. I suppose her magic made me feel I needed to allow her to use my office as a portal."

I recalled the portals Scarlet used to create as The Keeper of Stories. She'd move about the human world with the help of this skill. A skill I'd never learned since the hood's responsibility had fallen to me.

I shook my head. "No, I mean did you believe in her so much that you'd have done anything she asked without thinking?"

"No."

Unlike his usual thoughtful answers, he immediately confirmed he'd never felt compelled by her. I debriefed him on what the Wizard of Oz had shared with us about the god-like author theory, the manuscripts inside the rift, and the beginning of Storyland's error when an author somehow sent a real girl to live the alternate reality of a character in a book. Finally, I explained the characters' behavior in Storyland and how they had not only listened to me but had teleported to fulfill my demands instantly.

"The weird part is that it worked on the wolf," I said.

Reese scraped his fingers against the scratchy patches of hair on his chin. "I suppose as a former Keeper of Stories you must have influence over characters. It might be worth it to test the theory here. Tell me to do something."

"What?"

"Tell me to do something," he repeated. "I'm a character."

"Okay." I gestured with my bandaged hand. "Stand up."

Reese didn't move other than the flinch of his eye where heavy skin bagged at the bottom.

"Um. Touch your nose."

Kai laughed. "You didn't say 'Simon Says' first."

"Shush." I snapped at him before focusing specifically on Reese's story of *The Hunchback of Notre Dame*. "Okay what about this?" I looked him square in the eyes and called him by his character's name. "Quasimodo, go to Esmeralda and tell her that if you can't have her, no one else can either."

Nothing.

Nothing but the usual twitch of his eye responded.

"Well, that didn't work," I said. "I guess I'm not an all-powerful Keeper of Stories."

Kai shrugged. "Maybe not here. But if your gun works in our world and that works on characters in their world. Maybe it depends on Storyland."

It was a good theory, but not one we had time to test now. Since the gun worked here, I could rely on a load of bullets to stop the wolf. I silently thanked my former self for resisting the temptation to take the hood from where it was mingled with the rift's magic. Since I'd removed it from my body and thrown it onto the rift, everyone—every character and The Keeper of Stories included—had lost their immortality that came with protecting the story's ending. Once upon a time, characters could not die or be killed unless it was by a means that was written into their tale's plot. Now, we were free to shoot the wolf between the eyes, or rather *eye*, until he finally fell.

The fact that he bled was enough proof that we only needed more bullets and to aim each at his skull. Maybe even silver bullets. I'd bring him down before he hurt anyone… provided he didn't hunt anyone tonight.

"Thank you, Reese," I said, finally ready to set my determination to the side and get a little rest. I slid off the table and planted my feet on the floor with Kai steadying my good elbow. I looked up into his warm eyes and soaked in his natural musk. After eight days of walking through battlefields and fighting off a wolf, he smelled of sweat and dirt and himself and though he wasn't shower-fresh, I liked it loads more than the sterile sting of the morgue's bleach. "Let's go home."

We said our goodbyes to Reese and heaped on a few more expressions of gratitude before Kai helped me shuffle out the door and into San Francisco's nightlife. The chill of the late hour invited fog into the streets that seeped through my sweater with a lingering wetness. Despite the cold, my spirits lifted. I'd take car exhaust and cold nights over supernatural tornados any day. The lighter feeling helped carry me home as I picked up the pace and hurried to see our children.

As soon as I planted a kiss on Wendy's forehead and gave Jack a squeeze, I'd collapse into bed and get enough sleep to think clearly tomorrow. Tomorrow night I'd find the wolf who ate my fingers and kill him, but tonight, I'd rest and snuggle my babies.

After all, rest and recovery were the doctor's orders.

Chapter Thirteen

"And sleep, that sometime shuts up sorrow's eye, Steal me awhile from mine own company."

> — William Shakespeare, A Midsummer Night's Dream

Home smelled of soured baby bottles, Chinese takeout, and the bitter hint of taurine from too many half-consumed energy drinks. I breathed deeply as soon as we stepped inside. The warmth of the enclosed space wrapped around me like a welcome hug and the mess greeted me with the comfort of normalcy. The thought of sitting crisscross applesauce on the floor to fold onesies and underwear filled me with giddy excitement. To crank a podcast or a song from The Cranberries on my speaker while I scrubbed the dishes, was a luxury I wanted to sink into.

If only I could clean the mess of Storyland with a sponge and a vacuum.

We didn't dare flick on the light and disturb the lump on the couch. I squinted at the shape of Carlos curled across the cushions with one hand on the bassinet he'd dragged from the bedroom. Though his eyes looked closed, he continued rocking the portable crib with gentle sways.

Loud snores that could rival a chainsaw came from behind the couch where Scarlet lay sprawled on an air mattress large enough to cover our entire dining area floor. Why she'd chosen the temporary mattress over using our bed, I had no idea. It couldn't be comfortable to sink a nearly 9-month-pregnant body into a mattress made of air, but Scarlet often made odd decisions, like sprinkling cinnamon on potatoes or intentionally misquoting idioms.

As if hearing my thoughts, Kai's silhouette shrugged before he spun around and marched through the kitchen, turning left for the main bedroom.

I shook my head at Scarlet and let my shoulders sag, relieved she was sleeping soundly, and safe from the witch who'd escaped Story-land. I quieted rising fears of Mother Gothel and the wolf by slowing my breaths and focusing on the surrounding details.

Our tall table and four tavern-style chairs had been shoved to the front wall. Beyond Scarlet's temporary bed, white shutters were angled just enough to block most of the city's glow and the moonlight from streaming in through the sliding glass door. The stark light broke through in thin slits that lined the room.

I tiptoed around the coffee table which had been pushed to the center of the living room and piled with baby wipes, empty energy drink cans, a styrofoam takeout box, and my stack of study books with a few notes stuck to the edges. My scribbles kept track of the Grimm gods' suggestions. Tomorrow I'd go over the notes again with refreshed eyes and new information.

For now, I peered inside Jack's bassinet. He was swaddled in a yellow and blue crocheted blanket given to us by Kai's mother. The oversized blanket was the only one large enough to wrap around this chart-topping four-month-old.

"Five-month-old," I whispered, realizing that in the eight days we'd been gone, Jack had hit a new age milestone. Tears welled to the surface of my eyelids and stung just enough to dull the aches that still plagued me.

I brushed my thumb over his soft cheek and resisted the urge to scoop him into my arms or kiss his forehead. When Jack slept peacefully in his own crib, you didn't disturb him. *You just don't.*

I tore myself away and hurried out of the living room, through the little kitchen, and to Wendy's room. Since I didn't want to wake her, I only peeked through the crack in the door. My heart skipped a beat at the rosy shade that tinted the white bed frame, the cream carpet, and the yellow walls with magenta. I blinked and blinked, willing for Puck's love potion to go away before I came to my senses and spotted the ballerina night-light plugged into an outlet on the wall beside Wendy's nightstand. The tiny dancer was draped in a soft pink dress and matching pointe shoes that had cast a similar color across everything else in the room.

After patting my chest to calm down, I whispered through the crack, "I love you." I dragged myself into the bedroom where Kai was already dragging his shirt over his head. He'd swapped his jeans for plaid pajama pants and fell into bed shirtless.

He buried himself in the plush comforter while I slipped into an old pair of Christmas pajamas with skiing penguins. It took an extra minute to maneuver into the loose clothing without too much movement from my injured shoulder. I draped the sling on the knob of the nightstand's drawer and swore to wear it tomorrow.

Finally at ease, I crawled into bed, under the cover of the comforter and into Kai's open arms. With my head tucked below his chin and his arm beneath my neck, sleep came fast.

I woke to the greasy smell of bacon and with a growl in my stomach. Kai was gone, leaving behind a dented pillow and tangled sheets. I rolled away from the empty side of the bed and was welcomed by a tall glass of orange juice and a plate with a fluffy golden biscuit, two strips of bacon glistening with fat, and two over-easy eggs. The smiling face made with the egg yolks and the curved bacon was evidence of Kai's personal touch as well as the two pain-killer pills lined up next to the glass. I snagged the pills and popped them into my mouth before downing the orange juice.

In a few minutes, the effects would kick in and I'd have relief from the constant aching.

I felt like Frodo Baggins when he woke in Rivendell in *The Return of the King* movie. I half-expected Scarlet and Kai and Wendy to burst through the door for a quick jump on the bed.

To my absolute delight, it didn't take long for the daydream to be fulfilled. Before I could swing my legs to the side of the bed, the door flew open and Wendy bounded in. She threw herself onto the bed at my side and I enveloped her in a bear hug with a thousand kisses on the crown of her head. Though my shoulder throbbed along with my bandaged hand and the scabs on my arms were black with bruises, I ignored all the pain and focused on my daughter, taking care to keep my left arm from moving too much. I buried my face in the messy tangles of her bed-head hair and soaked in every second of cuddles.

After the snuggle reunion, she looked up at me, arching her neck so she could still keep her arms around my middle. "Did you fix the portal?"

The light in her eyes dimmed when my expression revealed that we hadn't. "Not yet," I said, "but soon, and we might have to borrow Auntie Scar."

Wendy frowned. "I don't think you want to do that. Auntie Scar is grumpy. You're always telling me not to whine but she whines all the time about how her belly hurts her back and the baby kicks her until she..." she stopped herself and lowered her voice to a whisper. "She pees her pants, Mommy."

I stifled a laugh.

"It's true!" She insisted. "One time when she sneezed, we had to leave the Girled Cheese early so she could go home and change her pants."

Still biting my tongue, I only smiled in response. Kai trailed in with a fresh face and wet hair. He wore a clean button-up with the sleeves rolled to his elbows and a pair of khakis that hugged his rear. My smile grew at the sight of him.

"You made breakfast?" I asked.

He laughed. "No way. I was way too lazy for that today. The Girled Cheese serves brunch now." He pointed to the plate. "See how the biscuit has a slice of cheddar in the middle? They also make a lot of breakfast sandwiches now."

"Brunch?" I sat up and Wendy slid off of the bed. "What time is it?" My phone wasn't where I usually left it on the nightstand. I must have been too tired to pull it out of my pants last night and plug it into the charger.

"Almost noon."

"Almost—Kai!" I squealed and scrambled out of bed. He folded his arms and leaned against the door frame, entirely too calm for my liking. I gritted my teeth and shot him an annoyed look. "You let me sleep that long when the wolf is on the hunt?" Not to mention Mother Gothel. A shiver stole through me and the calm awakening I had this morning was all but gone.

It was a new day, and we had a lot of research to do.

Again with the thought-reading, Kai avoided my spoken question. "You can slow down. Scarlet and Carlos requested that you rest and proceed with caution—for everybody's sake." his gaze flickered to my injured shoulder. "They're at the library going over historical texts and cross-referencing them with fairy tales and classic literature. You know how Scar hates to use the internet for research. And I've already started diving into the history of *The Little Cloak Girl*. No clear author yet but I've linked the timeline and the place of origin for the tale's first mention that I can find. It could be Edmund Spenser, John Donne, or even Shakespeare. They were all around England in the sixteen hundreds—"

I raised my hand to stop him. "Slow down. Let me get dressed and see my son first."

Despite my interruption, my husband grinned and stepped into the room. He opened his arms and pulled me to his chest, careful not to put too much pressure on my shoulder. "Aww, I'm so proud of you, my little eight-fingered friend."

"Don't you dare," I said, though I didn't care about the finger comment. I gave him a sly smile, feeling more energy and hope than I had in a long time. The wolf had cornered me, pinned against the ground in a strange land and I was alive to tell the tale. I was alive and ready to seal the rift. The best part of all was that it likely didn't require my sacrifice because my decisions as Red Riding Hood weren't the source of the errors.

"Too soon?" He pulled back so I could see his smirk.

I waved my bandaged hand and shrugged. "Nah, I meant don't call me your friend unless you're going to give me some benefits."

His head fell back as he laughed again and then returned his gaze to me. "But seriously, the fact that you're telling *me* not to rush is a good sign. Another day or two of healing and we'll return to the wild hunt."

"Ew," I said, "don't call it that."

"Right, right." He nodded. "The Wild Hunt is mythological folklore and folklore is a sore spot. Also, we are *best* friends but those benefits will have to wait until Jack's nap and when we put on a TV show for Wendy."

I agreed and slipped past him into the kitchen. Jack was cradled in a baby bouncer on the floor in the center of the kitchen. He was too big for it and could easily reach the overhead toys that hung from the attached bar. When he grabbed an elephant, the poor plastic animal iced over with frost and then split right off the bar where it hung. Jack brought it to his mouth and chomped down on the chilled toy.

I crouched and smoothed thin wisps of hair back from his forehead. "You're a smart guy, aren't you?" I said, cooing at him as he beamed up at me. "Yeah. You're smart to give yourself a cold teething toy like that."

He chewed the icy plastic in his gummy smile and giggled in response. After I fueled up and spent an hour snuggling Jack and listening to Wendy's stories, I requested Kai's help in the shower.

I kept my arm in place while he washed my hair and we even snuck in a moment of marital benefits behind closed doors. Armed with a sling, the gun reloaded and tucked into the holster beneath a fresh change of clothes, and painkillers in my system, we packed up the kids and readied for a brisk walk to the library. I stored my former

Post-It note collection with scribbled theories and thoughts into a spiral-bound notebook and placed it in the basket at the bottom of Jack's stroller.

Outside, the city greeted us with the wail of a siren and the sun peeking through a crack of cloud cover. I cupped the three good fingers over Wendy's hand while Kai pushed the stroller.

By the time we made it down to the street, the sun had burned off most of the gray and coated us with warmth. But the comfort of the sunshine didn't ward off all the shadows. Tall buildings still cast darkness into alleyways, and I found myself looking over my shoulder at every street corner, expecting to see two yellow eyes.

Of course he wasn't here, the wolf was waiting in the woods for Red. At least that was what I tried to tell myself. Had the beast really listened to me? And how long would his unexplained obedience last? If he behaved like the last wolf from *Little Red Riding Hood*—my coworker who had turned into a serial killer and a furry beast at the behest of the story aura—he'd only hunt at night.

I sucked in air through circled lips and noted the lack of yellow eyes and scraping claws. If nothing else, I could take comfort knowing that he was hunting me, not hunting Wendy or Scarlet. I glanced down an empty alley shadowed by an office building and found nothing but a couple of dumpsters. No wolf.

Finally, I relaxed and loosened my grip on Wendy. Since my phantom fingers already throbbed, I didn't need to add to the pain in my hand by squeezing the life out of hers.

Wendy's ponytail dipped back as she looked up at me. "You're not scared anymore?"

It took me a moment to understand what she meant. I lifted our hands and shook my head. "I'm not scared anymore because I have you."

"But you're the one who keeps people safe," she said, referring to the way I had explained my job to her in the past. "I'm going to be just like you."

"You're going to be an investigative journalist when you grow up?"

She shook her head, and the ponytail nearly smacked her in the face. "Nope! I'm going to be a writer and my stories will tell everyone how to not die."

I nodded and smiled. "That's very noble. Immortality According to Wendy Rowan?"

She shrugged, already distracted by a shiny display of jewelry in a shop window.

How had I spent years tormented by stories and the implications of immortality while my child wanted to center her life around them? At least if I failed at everything else in my life, I'd raised a fearless daughter. I gave her hand one more quick squeeze, hoping to soak up some of that fearlessness, because as soon as the sun set I'd have to hunt the wolf.

For now, and in the daylight, I relished the sun's warmth and Wendy's bravery.

Chapter Fourteen

"Are you not a Great Wizard?"

— L. Frank Baum, The Wonderful Wizard of Oz

Every detail of San Francisco—of the human world—pulled me into fragmented daydreams. When we passed the corner coffee shop, I pictured myself at the table by the window, sipping a latte and writing an article for my job at Bay Side Media. If I still had a job after my extended maternity leave. I wouldn't be surprised if my boss, Pam, replaced me with another crime reporter. The situation was made worse when Scarlet had taken my place as the company's secondary investigative journalist and then she went on maternity leave too, leaving Bay Side Media in a pinch.

Kai lifted the stroller over the thick bump of the curb and we continued past a row of towering office buildings. As mundane as the box windows and gray walls were, I found myself drawn to the offices while I imagined a scheduled day of typing, meetings, and pantsuits. I wanted a routine of school drop-offs and work mornings where I didn't have to worry if a wolf was hunting me or my daughter. I wanted to return to my life as a journalist, as a reporter who dug for the truth about crime in the big city and put it on display for all the mothers, women—people—to see. I wanted to warn innocent people about the dangers lurking in the alleyways so they could keep their families safe.

But that life was an eternity away. Unless we could separate *Little Red Riding Hood* from *The Little Cloak Girl* and the stories finally reincarnated with the correct plotlines, I'd spend my life hunting villains while human criminals slipped through the cracks and crime multiplied. Both the story aura and the escaped characters would double the amount of antagonists in our world all because Red was nowhere to be found.

We climbed the concrete steps to the library. Once inside, the rush of traffic and busy streets faded, and the library blanketed us in silence with the smell of books. I smiled at the librarian behind her desk on the right and then maneuvered through the maze of round tables in the center. We scanned the aisles of tall bookshelves for Carlos and Scarlet until we spotted them at the corner table in the back.

Tears sprang to my eyes at the sight of our friends. Scarlet bumped the table with her swollen belly and we wrapped our arms around one another. We ignored the stack of books that the bump knocked off the table. They fell to the ground with a thud and someone shushed us from one aisle over.

"I'm so glad you're alive," she said into my ear.

"Me too."

When we pulled away, I wiped my eyes and looked at her pregnant middle. "How did it feel to practice parenthood?"

Her shoulders slumped, and she puffed a breath out to blow a lock of curls from her tired eyes. "Awful," she said. "But I think I'll actually survive it now. I mean…" she waved her hand at Wendy who was peering into the stroller. Wendy dared Jack to grab her mini carton of chocolate milk so that his winter magic could turn it into a frosty treat. "If I can handle two kids, then one will be a piece of pie, right?"

"You intentionally say phrases wrong to irritate me, right?" I answered her question with a question.

Scarlet cocked her head but the hint of a smirk told me she knew exactly what I was referring to. "Fine. Raising Rapunzel will be a piece of cheesecake compared to your circus."

I rolled my eyes. "I see you haven't decided on a real name yet."

"What's wrong with Rapunzel?"

I gave her a deadpan stare and folded my arms. "Hmm. I don't know. How about the fact that the real Mother Gothel stepped through a freaking portal and wants to kidnap your child and that name will forever remind you of that threat?"

A woman scanning the books nearby shot us a look with wide eyes. I offered an awkward smile, and she shuffled away, shooing her son in the opposite direction.

Scarlet scoffed and let her arms hang limp in front of her. "Whatever. Maybe I'll name her Cloak Girl after her mommy."

I arched my eyebrow. "Good one. And when she learns to walk, she'll take your place in Storyland and fix your error?"

"Hey!"

That earned our crew another shush and a dirty look from the librarian who'd marched to the back corner just to check on us.

Scarlet lowered her voice. "You're seriously blaming me?"

"No." I shook my head. "I'm blaming your author. How the hell did you get into Storyland to become a character in the first place?"

She shrugged and blew out another breath that knocked her red hair away from her face. "That's the million dollar question, isn't it? I remember the woods. I remember the hunter. And I remember wandering and wandering and wandering. Then Red was there, and I just knew what to do."

"You and Red existed at the same time?"

She winced and rubbed her open hand over her stomach. A little groan escaped her. "We must have. Mari, I don't have the details anymore. I swear all that training and studying I did to become an investigator knocked the rest of the past out of my brain to make room."

I snapped my fingers, and we finally took a seat at the table. "That changes things. The Wizard of Oz swore the Cloak Girl replaced Red."

"Kai told us that had happened in Storyland," she said. "Surely we could have both existed in the human world together? I mean..." Her eyes scanned me up and down. "We have before." The reference to my time as Red Riding Hood sent shivers down my spine. I didn't want to recall how it felt to cut myself out of the wolf's belly.

"That's true...we did." My mind raced with theories. "So you somehow got into Storyland and the author wrote you a tale. But not until after you disturbed *Little Red Riding Hood*?"

Scarlet dipped forward, cupping her belly with both hands and then she took a long breath before she launched into a response. "Possibly. *The Little Cloak Girl* is hardly a story though. It's basically a ripoff of Red's tale except without grandma and the wolf. She lost her parents in the woods and then a hunter promised her they'd return. But they never did because the story wasn't finished."

I sank back into the hard chair and blocked out the murmur of Carlos and Kai discussing history. Wendy entertained Jack who froze her drink and Scarlet stared at me impatiently while I mulled over the clues.

"A ripoff of Red's tale..." I repeated. "A better version."

"Better?" Scar scoffed. "It doesn't even have an ending."

I straightened, suddenly scooting to the edge of my chair. "Right. Because Red's ending is tragic. She's eaten, dead, gone, but the Cloak Girl gets to live forever."

"If you call wandering around *living*," she said and then gasped. The sound came out sudden and louder than library rules would allow. Her outburst earned several dirty looks from meandering patrons until their gazes dipped to her stomach and their expressions softened.

Carlos jumped to his feet and insisted he retrieve her bottled water from the drugstore down the street.

I reached across the table and laid three fingers on her forearm. "Are you okay? Are you having contractions?"

Her cheeks puffed up like a chipmunk, and then she released a hard breath. "Yeah, I'm tired of these teasers. I wish they were real contractions, and I'd finally get to meet—" Before she said the name, she cut herself off and glanced at me. "My daughter."

With her relaxed again, my mind returned to Red. What had the

Brothers Grimm said about fairy tales? "Stories are warnings, they're lessons, they're teachers." Words stumbled over one another as if the thoughts couldn't get out of my mouth fast enough. "That has to be the key—the difference between Red's tale and the Cloak Girl's story."

"So *The Little Cloak Girl*'s message was 'get lost and you won't die'? That sounds terrible."

"No, no, I'm saying there wasn't a message because the story was written to replace Red," I said. "Or retell Red's story at least without the tragic ending."

"Some retelling," she said with a snort. "No grandma. No wolf. Where's the drama? Where's the excitement?"

"That's the point." I waved my bandaged hand. "There was no drama because I bet the author was trying to save you from dying in Storyland! They didn't finish the story so that you could wander your way out and come back here where you ran into the story aura version of Red."

My heart beat faster as the clues came together.

According to the Grimm gods and my research, *Little Red Riding Hood* was the only tale that existed across time and space but was virtually the same with every retelling. Red's story spanned cultures and in each one, her tale stood as a warning for people to watch their backs—*don't go into the woods alone and be careful who you trust*. Every fairy tale had a message and this one…this one was the only one repeated in the human world almost the same way the stories reincarnated in their own land.

And this one had chosen me.

Did I need to take Red's steps while Scarlet followed *The Little Cloak Girl*'s plot?

A clue resurfaced in my memory, and I swiveled in the squeaky chair. I ducked to grab the notes and books from the stroller's basket and then plopped them on the table. I plucked the sticky notes from their places inside the spiral bound pages and turned them around to show Scarlet.

"The Grimm gods believed I wasn't chosen to become Red," I said as I pointed to the scribbled note that I'd recorded in their words. *The story aura didn't choose you, Mari Fable, you chose the story. You differ from the other characters, and when you thwarted the tale's ending with a twist, you proved it.* The night they'd told me that, I'd taken the words right out of their mouths. They'd said it, but I was writing furiously, trying to quote them exactly so I could have precise notes. And somehow, I'd written faster than they'd spoken. It'd felt like a fever dream until now. "How could I have chosen the story if I didn't even know fairy tales were real? Was I always meant to be Red?"

Scarlet rubbed her open palm over her belly and scrunched up her face. For a moment, we both sat in silence as we tried to wrap our brains around the meta-level mystery.

"I don't know. Are you suggesting you act as Red while I act as the Cloak Girl and we make the events happen as they should?" she asked and then she scooted to the edge of the chair. "Wouldn't that require you to be eaten?" Her gaze flickered to my missing fingers, evidence that the wolf could injure me in Storyland even though I was a human from this world.

A pang cut through my chest, and bile swelled to the back of my tongue. I grimaced at the bitterness of the digested orange juice and biscuit. I refused to look at the precious family I'd leave behind if I had to become Red again.

They made my avoidance of them easier when Wendy announced she had to go to the bathroom and Kai offered to walk her there. Their footsteps faded, and I was left with Jack who snored softly from his stroller.

"Mari? Are *you* okay?" Scarlet asked, sensing my internal struggle.

After all this time, after all the hunting and articles and fairy tales I still found myself at the center of the same dilemma. Should I sacrifice myself to the wolf to seal the rift and end Storyland's influence over our world once and for all? Memory of the wolf's rancid breath, his bloodthirsty saliva, and the look of hunger in his eyes came back in a rush. I swallowed to force the vomit back down my throat.

Scarlet squeezed her eyes shut and gasped. When the Braxton

Hicks contraction passed, she pointed to a book on the floor. "That one," she said between breaths, "mentions *The Little Cloak Girl*."

I leaned over and grabbed the tome titled *An Incomplete History of Fairy Tales and Folklore*. I flipped through the pages, scanning the text until I found the Cloak Girl's section.

The Little Cloak Girl *originated at the same time as the first iteration of* Little Red Riding Hood. *Experts have identified recurring details in both stories including but not limited to: a red hood or cloak, a young girl traveling through the woods, precise instructions and warnings from the protagonist's parents, and a hunter who offers her advice. It is believed that* The Little Cloak Girl *is an unfinished version of* Little Red Riding Hood *and that the source of the first iteration of* Little Red Riding Hood *and the only iteration of* The Little Cloak Girl *is the same.*

The dry wording was snooze-inducing, and I covered my mouth as it split into a yawn. I continued reading down to the footnote at the bottom of the page. *Reference:* The Author of All, *a collected study of the similarities across fairy tales and classic literature throughout history.*

The *Author of All*? If I didn't know better, I might believe the Wizard of Oz himself had written and published this so-called study. Could L. Frank Baum have written it? Or maybe the author of Sherlock Holmes had a say in it, considering Sherlock was the one who had shared this theory with the wizard. Was the singular author theory a belief based on real clues or simply a conspiracy created by confused writers?

I tapped the page and hummed. "Have you seen a book called *The Author of All*?"

Scarlet nodded, and the chair squeaked when she stood. "I saw it on the shelf—" Her hand shot to her mouth as she stifled a gasp and her eyes bulged. "I think I just peed my pants."

My gaze flicked to her pants where a wet spot was spreading, slowly soaking her maternity jeans. The darkness on the fabric grew quickly—too quickly. I mirrored her with my hand over my gaping mouth and the gauze bandages nearly stuck to my lips. "Are you still peeing? Can you hold the rest?"

The wetness spread down the pant legs and Scarlet dipped forward, dropping her open palms on the table. She steadied herself and breathed through another contraction with her eyes squeezed shut.

"Scar, I think your water broke."

She shook her head, eyes still closed as her hand ran up and down her belly. "I'm not ready." Another contraction sparked a gasp that turned into a moan. She bit her lip, but the moan grew into a soft squeal that drew the attention of the judgmental woman with her son at her side. When I challenged her with a glare of my own, she finally stopped staring.

I stood and used my three pathetic fingers to cup Scarlet's elbow and peel her grip off of the table. "No one is ever ready, but it's okay because you'll figure it out along the way."

Scarlet grabbed hold of me and I winced as her fingers curled tightly around my good arm. The grasp sent me back to the hostage situation with Jane and Juliet. I exhaled through the triggering memory, masking it as a supportive breathing exercise for Scarlet to follow.

"Lean on Jack," I said as I transferred her hand to the stroller. "I'll find Carlos."

With another squealing groan, Scarlet white-knuckled the stroller's handle.

"Another one already?" I asked. I should have known Scar's labor would be atypical considering she wasn't quite like the rest of us. Her body had survived centuries on this planet and time in Storyland, too. She was an unnamed character from *Rapunzel*, giving birth to a princess—a princess according to the story, at least.

I turned to bolt for the door and find Carlos, but Scarlet's arm shot out and snagged my shirt. The tug pulled on my sling and I yelped as my stiff arm jarred out of place, but I quickly swallowed the sound and fixed my face because I wasn't the one doubled over in another contraction.

Scarlet was bent forward, balancing herself on the stroller with one hand and wringing the life out of my shirt with the other.

Squinted eyes stared up at me and through gritted teeth she said, "Don't leave me." Each word came out in staccato bursts. "This is—" The agony of the contraction interrupted her. Rapid breaths helped her ease through the pain but she looked woozy and I certainly couldn't catch her if she swayed. Not with my lame arm and half-eaten hand. "Carlos." She groaned and squatted, her knees dipping beneath her.

"Scar." I bent and met her gaze, my bandaged hand on her back. "This baby is coming. Fast. We have to get to the hospital immediately." I bit my tongue before I spilled the beans about the unusual speed at which her labor was progressing. A woman about to give birth for the first time did *not* need to hear theories about how unprecedented hers could be. Not to mention the fact that this birth could spark Mother Gothel's search. As a character, I didn't doubt she would sense Rapunzel's birth.

Just what we needed. Another stalker. Another threat.

But Scarlet had survived more than I could imagine, more hunting and villain encounters than my pitiful few years as The Keeper of Stories. She—and baby Rapunzel—would survive this just fine. I sucked in air and infused my voice with as much confidence as I could muster. "Don't worry. We will find Carlos on the way out."

Finally, she nodded and let me help pull her up. Together, we straightened and shuffled through the maze of tables. Scarlet gasped louder than any gasp I'd heard before. The librarian looked up with sharp, angled eyes but softened when she spotted Scarlet supporting her stomach.

"We need a hospital," I said, as I pointed to the door so that the librarian would understand.

All eyes were on us, and the librarian jumped into action. She edged around the enormous desk and opened the door for us to shuffle through.

"Mari!"

I shot a glance over my shoulder to see Kai jogging toward us with Wendy in his wake. As usual, relief flooded me at the sight of him. With Kai here, I could pass Jack off to him and fully support my best friend through labor and delivery, because I sure as hell wasn't leaving her side now.

We hurried through the doors where the busy city bustled, too busy to notice or care about the groaning woman, the womb water that soaked her pants, and the wet spots left in our trail. It was a welcome reprieve from the combination of curious and annoyed gazes inside the library.

I turned to my husband and relayed the plan. "Will you take Jack and Wendy while I go with Scar?"

Kai nodded and then with a wry smile, stooped to pick up the stroller and carry it down the stone steps. "Don't pass out." He tossed the joke over his shoulder, referencing his own blackout during Wendy's birth.

Several yards away, Carlos spotted us by the library's double doors. He bolted down the sidewalk and leaped over half of the steps in a single bound.

Behind him in the distance, I spied someone in the shadows between the bank across the street and an office building. The figure didn't move like the rest of the city goers in their hurried state of shopping and business meetings. This person was waiting and watching us. I felt their gaze prickle over my skin and I squinted at the shadow between buildings.

Had the start of Rapunzel's birth been a beacon for Mother Gothel as I'd suspected? Was the witch here to claim the prize for her trade? Though neither Scarlet nor Carlos had made a deal to give their first-born for the witch's Rampion, the character likely still felt the story's pull to kidnap Rapunzel.

I frowned and searched the alley for any sign of movement.

Instead of the ruffled hem of Mother Gothel's dark layered skirts, a gray tail with matted fur melted into the shadows.

"Ebenezer Scrooge," I cursed.

The wolf is already hunting.

Chapter Fifteen

"Lord, what fools these mortals be!"

— William Shakespeare, A Midsummer Night's
Dream

Though Carlos insisted on calling a Lyft, an Uber, *and* a cab to see which car would arrive first, Scarlet refused to get in any of them until I mentioned the wolf. For her sake, I danced around the details, suggesting the possibility of his presence rather than the fact that I'd witnessed him stalking us.

All three ordered cars were parked in a line along the sidewalk but Scarlet shuffled past each one, headed for the hospital three blocks away.

"Scar, please," Carlos said. He gently laid his open palm at the square of her back and pointed at the Lyft with his free hand.

She shook her head. "I feel better walking."

The anxiety of first-time birth radiated from her and I picked up the pieces, absorbing the nerves from her quivering voice. I remembered how it'd felt to be bossed around by everyone. The father of the baby always told the mother to be calm, and though it was usually said with good intentions, it was just another useless instruction spouted at the woman in labor. Then came the doctors and nurses and hospital administration and mother-in-laws and whoever else felt the need to push advice onto the new mom while the new mom pushed out her baby. Of course doctors and nurses in a hospital far away from the wolf were exactly what we needed right now.

I glanced at the alley where the wolf had slunk away into the shadows. Though there was no sign of his glistening teeth or yellow eyes, I didn't doubt he was still watching us. I'd told him to wait for Red in the woods but it seemed he no longer listened. Of course a hungry beast didn't have the patience I'd hoped for, and he wasn't a serial killer selected by the story aura like the first wolf had been. I was wrong to have compared the two because this time he was the actual manifestation of the character from Storyland. He didn't follow the "rules" of the story aura.

Stupid, stupid, stupid. I silently chastised myself for assuming this wolf would behave the same as the other had. My fingers found the hard metal of the weapon tucked beneath my shirt. If nothing else, at least I had brought bullets as backup.

"Scarlet," I said as I jogged to catch up with her surprisingly quick steps. When I jumped in front of her, it forced her to stop. "I know it feels better to pace and get the jitters out but you'll end up delivering this baby in the middle of the city if you don't get into one of those cars. I'm only here to remind you that your birth plan was to be with the doctor you chose. So let's get you to your OBGYN faster." With my good arm, I waved my bandaged hand open as if to say *after you*.

She sighed and then grunted as another contraction pulsed through her. Her forehead glistened with perspiration until she swiped her sleeve across it. The moment ended with a breathless groan and she looked up at me through long lashes where beads of sweat clung to the tips. Finally, she rolled her eyes and relented. "As you wish," she quoted one of her favorite films through clenched teeth and turned to shuffle to the closest vehicle.

Carlos waved the other two ordered cars away after shouting a promise to send them good tips through their respective phone apps.

We piled into the car, flanking Scarlet who sat doubled over in the center seat.

Other than the tension of her contractions, the car ride went off without a hitch and I breathed easier knowing we'd put distance between us and the wolf. I comforted myself with the thought that he'd stayed in the shadows so far. There was no way he'd stalk into the bright lights and bustling halls of the hospital.

No way.

Carlos threw a dozen dollar bills at the driver and stumbled over a combined thank you and apology. He helped Scarlet out of the car whose fingernails sank into his skin. The sight of it had me seething, though she hadn't touched me.

Behind us, the hospital's doors slid open and patients hurried in and out. I mirrored their impatience as I jogged toward the labor and delivery wing. As the doors slid open again, a rush of conditioned air hit me with the smell of bleach. I wrinkled my nose and headed for the administration desk with Scarlet and Carlos only a few steps behind.

The lobby was busy with patients being wheeled in and out either in labor or leaving with their bundles of joy wrapped in their arms. I scanned the area for a wheelchair but Scarlet didn't need it yet. She continued pacing by the doors, practically dragging Carlos along with her as she stared wide-eyed at another mother who peacefully cooed at her newborn baby.

I remembered the odd combination of envy and fear when other parents passed by with their infants. I'd wanted to meet my children so badly that waves of jealousy had surfaced when I saw mothers further along than me. Not to mention the desire to be done with pregnancy and past the unknowns of giving birth. No doubt Scarlet was feeling the same.

I patted the countertop, eager for the employee to get us into a labor and delivery room. The whoosh of the doors sliding open sent a rush of cool air at my back. Buried in the white noise of conversations, I caught a low, rumbling growl. I spun around, back pressed against the tall countertop at the administration desk and scanned for yellow eyes, or a tail, anything that resembled the beast.

A man marched in through the doors, confident and cool until his head snapped to me. His brow furrowed. My gaze dropped to the visitor's badge around his neck and my eyes narrowed on the name. Did it say Jameson? I blinked rapidly and squinted as he passed by me.

It read *Andrew Jones*. I blew out a breath and gently patted my cheek. "Back to reality, Mari. The wolf is from Storyland. He's not Jameson." I knew this was the truth, but it didn't ease my thundering heart or settle the storm in my gut.

Everything about this moment felt all too familiar, as though I'd lived it in a past life and I was merely repeating the same story. If the events played out as they had the last time I'd heard a wolf's howl in the labor and delivery wing, I could predict what came next. Scarlet's daughter would go missing after being kidnapped at the hands of a strange woman. But I was no oracle or seer or misfortune teller and this would not happen. I'd never let this happen.

Still, I couldn't shake the feeling that I knew what was coming. I knew *who* was coming.

"Excuse me?" A woman's sugary-sweet voice interrupted my sanity pep talk. She'd returned our IDs and Scarlet's medical insurance card to the counter and then slid two visitor's stickers toward me. "There's a room ready for Ms. Scarlet. Fill these out and wear them so that you can accompany the patient."

I thanked her and shoved thoughts of the wolf away. Today was about my best friend and her new baby, not fairy tales… I prayed to the Grimm gods—no, to the mysterious "Author of All" that Storyland and its characters would leave us alone just for today.

I swallowed the lump in my throat, forcing my heart to slow down as I beckoned Carlos and Scarlet to the double doors.

We pushed through the swinging doors and were greeted by a nurse who guided us to a small room. She filled out Scarlet's chart while instructing her to change into a hospital gown. I encouraged Scarlet to lean on me and steady herself while Carlos helped her peel the wet pants from her legs and pull the gown over her head.

"Go ahead and lay back on the bed," the nurse suggested.

Scarlet snapped back with a refusal and continued pacing.

I offered the nurse a smile and stepped up, appointing myself Scarlet's birth advocate. "Don't worry, her bark is worse than her bite," I said, joking just enough to butter up the nurse who'd likely be with us for the next couple of hours. "We're grateful for the recommendation, but part of her birth plan is to stay walking as long as possible through the labor." I figured honey caught more flies than vinegar and Scarlet's birthing team would need a little extra sweetness to get through this. But the idiom left a sour taste in my mouth. Barking and biting were two activities that brought my anxious mind right back to the beast who hunted me.

Though the man hadn't been Jameson and the real wolf was in our rearview mirror, it was possible he'd track us here. I didn't want to lead a monster right into Scarlet's peaceful birth plan. *Should I leave?* I glanced at the door that fell shut as the nurse left to retrieve Scarlet's OBGYN.

Memories of Wendy's birth flooded my mind. Of the doctor I'd imagined with fangs when the story aura had been dancing around me, just about to plague me with *Little Red Riding Hood*'s plot. Of the horrifying moment that my daughter went missing after Scarlet herself had whisked the newborn babies away into another room on another floor. Of the sickening guilt I'd felt when I couldn't recognize my daughter among the other hours-old infants.

"I have to push," Scarlet shouted. She was doubled over, white-knuckling the end of the bed frame with a slight bend in her knees.

"Your doctor is on his way," Carlos said while he rubbed her back.

Adrenaline kept me standing but watching my best friend suffer left my head spinning. I mimicked a mother in labor and breathed in through my nose and forced the air out in a long exhale until my woozy head came down from the clouds and the swishing nausea in my gut calmed.

Locks of hair soaked in sweat framed Scarlet's face as she stared at the tiled floor between her bare feet. I yanked the hair tie from my ponytail and scooted to her side, gathering her red curls into the thick elastic band. "I can't wait, Carlos!" She screamed.

"She's right," I told him. "If the baby is coming—"

Scarlet groaned in a long tight voice until her tone shifted to a shrill squeak. The doctor burst in and I jumped, nearly ripping a lock of Scar's hair out when it stuck to the gauze on my bandage.

She shot me an irritated look that only lasted a second before the doctor guided her to crouch on all fours. Two nurses quickly laid out sterile paper bed sheets beneath her as she sank to her hands and knees.

I folded my legs beneath me, sitting beside Scarlet and letting her shove her shoulder into my good side as she rocked back and forth on her knees.

The door swung open again as another nurse entered. The temporary exposure left goosebumps on my neck and collarbone. The brief view of the hallway was nothing but emptiness and stark white walls. Still, I sensed the prowling of a predator nearby. What if the wolf caught up with us? *What if he's here? I should leave.*

I tried to stand but Scarlet slapped the heel of her hand against my leg and pinned me down. "I don't have a name," she said between breaths. "My brain is stuck on Rapunzel. I need a name," she repeated.

"What about Ahri? I said, suggesting the first name Scarlet had wanted to call herself when she became mortal.

"Ahri?" She glanced up at me and I gave her my warmest smile. Her face flickered with either fear or pain. Could she sense my desire to leave? Or had her mention of Rapunzel sparked worry of Mother Gothel's approach? When the expression twisted and she released a scream, I chalked it up to the pain of labor. Despite the chaos, I kept thoughts of the wolf and the witch at the forefront of my mind. I needed to stay alert in case either tracked us here and became bold enough to enter the hospital.

"Breathe through it," the doctor said, "and then give me another big push."

Carlos brushed escaped hairs from Scarlet's face and with one more grunting push, a baby's cry drowned everything else out. The poor child likely wailed at the sudden cold of the hospital's conditioned air—an unpleasant contrast from the warm womb she'd just been bathed in.

Tears flooded Carlos's eyes and Scarlet sighed in a moment of relief. Their child was here, alive and well with a healthy set of lungs. The doctor offered a shining medical tool to Carlos who swallowed and gingerly accepted it. When he cut the cord, Scarlet sat back on her legs and the doctor shifted the baby into her mother's arms. In her mother's hold, the crying bubbled to a stop, and all was silent other than a few sniffles from Carlos.

Emotion swam in my gaze and a tear slipped down my cheek at the sight of Scarlet's beaming face. Her rosy cheeks were flush with joy and exhaustion and relief. She clutched her daughter's naked body to her chest and held her against exposed skin where the hospital gown had slipped off one shoulder.

Carlos wrapped his arm around her in a gentle hug and while Scarlet gazed in awe of their baby, he gazed in awe of Scarlet. It was the cutest darn sight I'd seen since Kai and Jack were dressed in matching blue shirts splashed with the words *gamer dude* across the front.

"Ahri?" Scarlet whispered. She brushed her cheek against the crown of her daughter's fuzzy head. The child's distinct red hair and furrowed expression marked her as the equal combination of Carlos and Scarlet. "Do you like that name?"

The baby responded with a faint gurgle that sparked a smile across Scarlet's tired, sweaty face. I rubbed her arm and congratulated her strength and on the arrival of Ahri.

After the brief calm, the doctor encouraged Scarlet to get ready to deliver the placenta, and a nurse scooped the baby from her arms. The door opened, flooding the room with bright light and sending a sudden shiver down my spine.

My head snapped up from the new parents to the woman in a long lab coat who'd slipped inside. While one nurse held Ahri, the other measured the baby's head and then checked her temperature with an ear thermometer. The pediatric doctor crowded in with the nurses and scooped Ahri from their hold. The doctor's frantic movements sent my heart skipping, and I slowly got to my feet.

"We need to weigh her," the nurse said, but the doctor didn't listen.

The doctor spun away from the rest of the medical team and

yanked open the door. "This baby is sick," she said. My stomach dropped. *Sick?*

Scarlet's head popped up. "What?"

"She needs help," the doctor said as she stepped out of the room. Before the door swung shut, a chorus of ear-splitting screams rippled through the hospital's hallways. Alarm bells exploded in my head, but not loud enough to drown out the growling.

No. Not now.

Though the doctor may have had the best intentions to help the sick baby, she was taking the child closer to danger.

Through the shouting and screaming, I heard the predator's call loud and clear. The wolf's howl rang through the hospital and my heart stopped.

Chapter Sixteen

"All you need is confidence in yourself."

— L. Frank Baum, The Wonderful Wizard of Oz

The beast's resonating voice echoed from deep within his belly, and I knew he was challenging me to come out and meet him. Horror clenched my heart as if his claws were bearing down on my chest again.

"My baby!" Scarlet shrieked.

My head swiveled, eyes unblinking to see my best friend choking on sobs. "I'll get her," I promised. With my good arm, I ripped the gun from the holster and held it at my side before slipping out the door.

The stark white hallway was a sea of panic as nurses ushered patients and visitors into rooms and then barred the doors. The wolf was nowhere to be seen but the screech of claws against steel announced he was near. Wide-eyed men and women shoved past me as I walked against the flow of traffic. They ran from the monster whose warning could cause a grown man to soil his pants. I scanned every person who passed by but none carried a grumpy redheaded baby.

"Where are you, Ahri?" I breathed as I arched to the balls of my feet and tried to find the doctor who'd taken her.

A panicked mother slammed into my recovering shoulder, and a yelp escaped me. A gnawing ache splintered from the sore joint, snaking up into my collarbone and neck until my entire right side throbbed. I chewed on my inner cheek to draw my attention away from the pain, and then I pushed my way to the end of the hallway.

Finally, I caught sight of the woman in a long white coat as she blazed a trail through the wheelchairs and past the nurses. Despite her tiny frame and slow movements, she'd made it through the crowd easier than I did. People respected her white doctor's coat and subconsciously moved out of her way to let her pass. Or perhaps they hadn't wanted to crush the hunched doctor and the tiny baby in her arms.

At the end of the hall, she turned, sensing my gaze. It was then I saw her face and recognized the hardened mouth and cold eyes. I froze as she paused in front of the elevators and challenged me to a staring contest across the hall. The unsettling curve of her wrinkled lips was a sign that she believed she'd won.

I dodged a wheeled bed in the hallway as the elevator doors slid open. Mother Gothel disappeared inside the elevator, her long dark skirts brushing the floor with every step. Ahri's dry, helpless scream shattered my heart, and I ran for the elevator, but not quickly enough. The doors dinged and Mother Gothel held her smirk as the elevator closed.

"No!" I slammed the heel of my hand against the button in the wall. The gun nearly slipped from my three-fingered grasp as I pressed the button over and over and over. "No, no, no!"

The red number above the door indicated the elevator was set to travel to the second floor. That stop might give me enough time to catch up, so I shifted to the next elevator and punched the button.

The wolf's growl tore my attention to the opposite side of the hallway where security guards clad in gray and black uniforms shoved their bodies against a heavy door. Above them hung a sign that marked the door as the path to the staircase.

All at once I knew Mother Gothel's plan. I knew she was using the wolf's killer instinct to her advantage. As chaos ensued, the witch would slip out of the hospital with Rapunzel and escape into Storyland while I was too busy fighting off a murderous beast.

Through the thin rectangular window, I saw a flash of matted fur and glistening teeth. The wolf slammed his claws against the door, strong enough to smash the steel inward. Jagged dents seemed to reach out and try to grab the security guards.

The wolf dropped to all fours as he spotted me through the glass. A single yellow eye stared into my soul and I swear his jaw split into a grin. That long red tongue flicked over black lips and a string of frothy saliva stretched from his chin until it dripped out of sight.

I broke our shared gaze and turned away. I had to go after Ahri. I had to keep my promise to Scarlet. The security guards were successfully keeping the floor of women and children safe. I'd return to bring him down if police officers didn't do it for me first. Guns worked just fine here, and I'd seen him bleed once before. Claws screeched against steel and the monster snarled, but I didn't let his threat distract me.

"I'm coming, Ahri," I whispered.

The elevator returned, and the doors spread, inviting me to step inside and follow the witch. Before the doors slid shut, I caught an announcement from one of the security guards. He told the others that animal control officers were on their way in a shaky voice. It wouldn't matter now. The wolf had already stopped scratching at the door and his growls silenced.

He was focused enough to follow me.

I released a string of curses into the quiet of the elevator where no one else could hear my defeated frustration. The wolf would beat me to the first floor, and I wouldn't dare lead the powerful creature toward Ahri. I didn't have time to go after Mother Gothel until I stopped him from attacking. I only hoped that the old witch's sluggish pace would give me enough time to catch up after I faced my enemy.

The thought of fighting the wolf again made my head light and dizzy, and my feet unsteady. I shut my eyes and tried to calm myself before the elevator stopped. After a weak breath—in through my nose, out through my mouth—I opened my eyes. I shrugged off the sling, leaving it on the ground beside my feet as I gripped the gun with both hands.

I slammed the second floor button with the back of my hand and the elevator came to a sudden stop. The red number turned to two and as soon as the doors opened, I jogged across the hall to the stairs. I pushed through the door and paused on the staircase landing.

Silence greeted me. *Where are you, Beast?* I almost wished for the growling and the scrape of his sharp claws. At least then I'd be able to identify his location.

I eased down two steps, still listening and waiting with the gun ready in my grip. The staircase was empty, devoid of life and sound until I spotted the steam of his breath through the slats of the steps above me. The shadow moved over my head as he descended the stairs.

"I told you to wait for me in the woods," I said. I raised my gun and positioned my feet wide enough to balance my weight between both legs.

The wolf huffed. "Your powers don't work here, Author."

Author?

He stopped on the landing above and it was clear he was large enough—strong enough, to launch himself across the entire flight of stairs and take me down. I raised my gun and aimed to put a bullet between his eyes. Several, in fact. "Why do you think I crossed over where you couldn't control me?"

"Why did you call me that?" I asked. His tongue slithered out and over his shining black nose. "I–I thought you would call me Red."

He blew a breath out through his nostrils, and his one eye blinked slowly. "The Author wrote themself into many of their stories. I've seen it with plenty of other characters. You are not special, Red."

His paw landed on the next step down and the muscles in his shoulders shifted, twitching around the spot Kai had shot him. The yellow eye blinked, and he bared his teeth. How many bullets would it take to bring him down?

My arms shook from holding the gun up for too long. I wanted to ask more and to understand why he'd called me an author—no, *The*

Author, but he was inching closer with all the confidence of both worlds.

"I'm not Red anymore," I said. "And I'm not an author." He only chuckled and my blood chilled. The sound was too human coming from a snout covered in fur and a mouth of fangs. "Stop or I'll take your other eye." I gripped the gun tighter and felt the cold steel against the flesh of my forefinger.

"I told you once already. Your storytelling powers do not work in a world where you are an author."

"Maybe not, but my gun does."

He was too close. Too confident at the other end of a barrel.

I pulled the trigger. The bullet caught at the corner of his mouth and it slowed him. I backed away, as far as I could on the second floor landing without moving onto a narrow step, and then I steadied my stance. He shook his head, expanding and closing his jaws as blood dripped from his lips. Red spotted the stairs in scattered droplets.

I blew out a breath and aimed again, firing at the crown of his skull this time. The shot ripped through his ear, causing him to pause and shake his head again. His snarl built into a roaring growl as he snapped at the air and lunged for me. I bit back a scream and fired again.

With another round of rapidly released bullets, the beast collapsed with a thud at my feet. My arms dropped while my heart thudded in my throat. My muscles shook and my shoulder ached something fierce. Despite the pain, relief washed over me and breath returned as my lungs finally expanded past fear's clutch.

I doubled over with the heels of my palms on my knees. Blood oozed from the gaping hole in the wolf's brow, soaking the fur until it turned dark and shiny. His body faded out of existence and back to Storyland, I suspected, where he'd reincarnate and return to hunt for a girl in the woods.

A door slammed somewhere higher in the stairwell, and voices filled the narrow space. On shaking legs, I made my way down the staircase and away from the shouts of officers in the landing above.

"The wolf went down there." The security guard's voice echoed against the white walls. Footsteps thundered like a storm overhead and

I picked up the pace, hurrying for the first floor as I tucked the gun back into my holster.

I burst through the exit and stumbled into the lobby. If I was lucky, a security guard had stopped Mother Gothel from leaving with somebody else's newborn. I scanned the lobby but found no trace of the witch. Outside the sliding doors, I soaked in the fresh air and let the wind dry the sweat from my forehead. The cool air stunk of car fumes but I relished the breeze and the open space.

Red blinkers flashed as vehicles turned into the drop off lane in front of the hospital. Past the cars, pedestrians and patients walked through the lot toward the labor and delivery wing or through the rows of parked sedans and SUVS. There was no sign of the witch's black layered skirts, and no shrill cry from Ahri.

They were gone.

I wanted to collapse on the concrete and fade away to Storyland like the wolf had. I sank to the curb along the drop off lane and dropped my head into my hands. Mother Gothel's plan had worked. She'd successfully kidnapped Rapunzel, stealing away the newborn baby right from under her mother's nose. I couldn't bear the thought of returning to Scarlet's room empty-handed because I knew exactly what it'd felt like to lose track of a child just after birth. Fear and guilt and shame gutted me now as deeply as it had when Wendy was taken from me.

I allowed myself a minute to take a breath before I pulled out my phone and dialed Carlos's number. The other line rang and rang until his voicemail answered. I tried two more calls to not avail. A sigh escaped me and I dropped my hand into my lap, resolving to get to my feet and get the bad news to the new parents.

My gut clenched, and I swallowed the urge to vomit. If I brought a plan to Scarlet, it would be easier to tell her I'd failed to retrieve Ahri. Could I walk into Storyland and demand Mother Gothel listen to me? How long would it take to find her? And what in the Wonderland had the wolf meant when he'd said I had powers? Was my control over the characters more complex than a simple belief in me? The questions overlapped and I couldn't keep my mind straight.

One thought kept returning, kept nagging me and maybe it was because of the footnote that had been lingering in the back of my brain. The reference to the *Author of All* combined with the Wizard of Oz and Sherlock's strange theory had me itching to research and understand this. Even the wolf seemed to know more than I did, and I never liked it when the villain—the suspect—knew more than I did.

Why the hell had he called *me* The Author?

Chapter Seventeen

"She is protected by the Power of Good, and that is greater than the Power of Evil."

— L. Frank Baum, The Wonderful Wizard of Oz

An SUV screeched into the drop off lane and tore me from my moment of grief and deep thought. I jumped away before the car bumped over the edge of the curb. A harried man leaped out of the driver's seat with the engine still running and ran over to the passenger door. I bit back a shout at his reckless driving as I watched him help a laboring woman from the front seat.

I let the irritation go and dragged myself back inside as quickly as I could. Scarlet deserved answers as soon as possible, but the labor and delivery wing was barred from visitors.

The employee at the administration desk offered me an apologetic smile. "You're welcome to wait until it reopens." She waved at a row of chairs to the left of the desk. "But I can't guarantee that will happen anytime soon."

"What's going on?" I asked, curious what the officers thought had happened to the wolf.

She gestured toward the sliding doors. "A wild animal got spooked into the hospital and then got stuck. The last I heard, animal control had it under control. They chased the creature out or something, I guess." I snorted, and she shot me a strange look. "Once we get the all-clear from law enforcement, we'll ease the security measures. The safety of our patients comes first."

"What about the missing baby?"

Her thick makeup crusted above her eyebrows as she wrinkled her forehead. She shook her head. "There are no missing children, Ma'am."

Based on the clarity in her eyes and the steadiness of her voice, this employee wasn't hiding what she knew, she was simply clueless. The hospital was likely unaware of Ahri's absence. To Scarlet's birthing team, it was another doctor who took the baby for checkups. Still, how could they let a baby get kidnapped right out from under their noses?

Frustration burned in my chest as the employee naively smiled at me.

I ran my tongue along my top teeth and then swallowed another rising urge to shout at an innocent person in my path. *I* was the one who'd failed, not this employee. I was the one to blame, not the harried driver and his laboring partner. I was the one who let the witch dressed up as a doctor slip away with Ahri in her arms.

"Okay, thanks." I forced a smile and waited until she turned back to the computer to side-step the administration desk. I knew the security guards were too busy to stop me so I slipped through the swinging doors and into a long white hallway.

Before any medical personnel saw me, I ducked into the elevators. The walk to Scarlet's room passed in a fog. I wasn't ready to enter, but I pushed through the door, anyway.

Carlos was on the phone, talking with animation as he flailed his free arm around and a vein bulged in his forehead. In the bed, Scarlet hugged a pillow against her chest and her swollen eyes were squeezed shut.

The door clicked to a close behind me and her eyes popped open.

Red lines cracked the whites of her eyes and her pale skin was splotched. Her lips parted, barely giving voice to her daughter's name.

I shook my head and tears welled in my eyes as I explained.

"Ahri wasn't sick because the doctor who'd said so wasn't a doctor at all," I started. "She was Mother Gothel." I crossed the room and gathered her hands in mine, ignoring the pain every time I moved my shoulder.

Tears spilled down her cheeks in a silent, gut-wrenching grief and I joined her, sobbing as I sank onto the mattress. I pressed my forehead against hers and we held one another crying until dehydration slowed our tears. I tried to find words but nothing would be enough so I simply told her the truth.

"She got away for now, Scar. And I know this is a lot to deal with right after birth, but I'll get her back."

"You have to go," she said between shuddering breaths as she pulled away from me. Her eyes shifted and narrowed, searching mine for the answer she wanted to hear. "You have to go, now."

"Scar, Mother Gothel would have made it to Storyland by now." Images of war, beheading, and dead mermaids flashed through my mind and raised goosebumps on the back of my neck.

The worst part wasn't even death because the stories and characters would reincarnate and live again to seek their purpose and try to follow their plots. The worst part was that the characters would never find their purpose, and they'd suffer over and over and over again until I figured out how to fix this.

Scarlet was the only answer we'd found, but she was in no condition to travel into Storyland and trace the mistaken steps she'd taken through Red Riding Hood's story. Without those steps, fairy tales would continue to tangle with confused characters while the story aura spilled over into San Francisco. The battle would never end and I was no longer the immortal Keeper of Stories who could spend an eternity correcting the errors and guiding the lost characters. As much as I'd wanted to intervene when the goats had smashed Cinderella's slipper or when Medusa had turned Guinevere to stone, it wouldn't have mattered. War would rage on as long as the characters lost their way and the story's messages were twisted.

I blinked and shoved the memories of Lancelot's lifeless stare away so that I could meet Scarlet's gaze with clear eyes. "I don't think I can handle going back alone. I need your help."

Her splotchy cheek was indented as she gnawed at the inside of her mouth. Sadness surrounded the glimmer of hope in her eyes and the strength in her grip told me she'd placed that hope in me. "Please, Mari. Mother Gothel is old and slow and she doesn't know how to navigate the human world as well as you do. You can catch up with her before she crosses over."

Shoot. Oxygen seemed in short supply, sucked from the room. Scarlet was right, and I was running out of time.

I reached for her hand around the pillow and gave her the best squeeze my three fingers could give. "I'll figure this out."

Scarlet managed a sad smile and a faint nod before she pulled her hand away and waved me toward the door. I slid off the bed and crossed the room in three long strides. As I tugged the door open, Scarlet's voice stopped me but I didn't turn around.

"I need my baby," she said, "and you're the queen of twisting stories. Don't let this end the way it was written."

I chewed on my lip, keeping my doubt to myself. The stories were already twisted, and it was the disruption of Red's original tale that had caused all of this. On top of that, I no longer wore the hood or had the Keeper's abilities to help me track characters. Who was I to rescue Rapunzel and change the course of what had been written?

After a quick nod, I crossed the threshold and let the door fall shut against my back. I couldn't let Scarlet see my lack of confidence. From the beginning, our plan was thin and based on a theory that we'd patched together with scrap pieces of a broken puzzle.

Despite my doubt, I picked up the pace and hurried from the hospital. If nothing else, I could delay Ahri's kidnapping and return the new baby to her mother until the witch inevitably showed up again.

In the lobby, the woman at the administration desk pointed at me as she saw me exit the hallway. "Hey! You weren't supposed to be back there during a lockdown—"

I let her shouts bounce off my back as I ran through the sliding doors and into the busy parking lot.

———

THE HIKE from the hospital to Pioneer Park crossed streets and sections of the city I knew better than my own living room. Shortcuts through alleyways helped me skip crowded intersections where crosswalk lights would take too long. No longer afraid of the wolf, I could slip in and out of the shadows without a starving stalker nipping at my heels.

Dusk had come, and with it the twinkling lights of the city at night. The earlier clouds had cleared and the warm glow of the setting sun beckoned me toward the park where pedestrians enjoyed evening walks or cut through the city on their way to visit San Francisco's shore. I turned onto Main Street and started the long climb up the steep road. At the top, couples walking dogs and joggers disappeared into the trees that lined Pioneer Park.

I huffed as I tried to keep a quick pace uphill and my eyes on the pathway that led into the park. I scanned Main Street for any sign of a woman in a white coat or dark, layered skirts. If Mother Gothel was truly as aged and as slow as she seemed, I should have caught up with her by now. The elderly witch might have magic, but she was frail, and holding a very angry baby.

The familiar pine scent of Pioneer Park greeted me as I turned and jogged down the closest path. At the end of the path, I spotted a small figure limping past the playground. The white streaks in Mother Gothel's charcoal braid identified her. Ahri had quieted now, possibly soothed by the rhythmic up and down sway of the witch's slow gait. Mother Gothel had shed her white coat somewhere along the way and her heavy black dress earned a few double-glances from a couple sitting on a nearby bench.

I slowed to a stop, catching my breath now that I knew I had Mother Gothel—and Ahri—within reach. Air couldn't fill my lungs fast enough. My chest squeezed with every sucked breath and I bent to balance my hands on my knees. The woman on the bench asked if I was okay so I shot the wide-eyed couple a quick thumbs up to assure them I didn't need an ambulance.

I was out of shape but I would not die after a little jog through the city. The gasping breaths turned into a dry, uncontrollable cough that tightened my throat. Okay, maybe running *would* kill me. What a way to go after years of tracking villains and surviving a walk through a war-zone.

As Mother Gothel drew closer to the flickering scrap of red in the center of Pioneer Park, I started moving again. I shuffled after her, dragging myself to reach her before she slipped into the alternate universe with my best friend's baby.

The witch plucked the hood's edge and began to peel it away from the rift.

"Stop," I said between gasps.

At the sound of my voice, the fabric slipped from her knobby fingers and she twisted her gaunt neck to glance over her shoulder. Her braid brushed over her other shoulder and her eyes shrunk to slits. When she opened her mouth, I grimaced at the sight of her black teeth and cracked pale lips. "This baby does not belong in the human world."

I took a step forward and reached for the bundle in her arms but Mother Gothel pulled away and tucked Ahri into her other side. "She doesn't belong with you either," I said.

The witch laughed a raspy chilling laugh and the cracks in her bottom lip split further, pulling blood to the surface of the dry skin. "Oh, but she does. This is my story, Grimm."

My heart sputtered at the name she'd called me. "Excuse me?"

"Look and see with the eyes of The Creator," she said as she turned and revealed the bundle in her arms "See what you have written and know this is what you have done. This is the only way and only the beginning for her."

A gasp slipped from me and my hand shot to my mouth at the sight of the still baby. Ahri's pink cheeks had turned blue and her tiny body, swaddled in a thin hospital blanket, looked stiff.

Tears blurred my vision. "Is–is she dying?"

"Rapunzel belongs with the other characters." The witch's foggy eyes met mine.

I shook my head, blinking back the tears. "No. She belongs with her mother."

Mother Gothel looked down at Ahri, but the baby's shade of blue did nothing to inspire compassion. Only determination and hunger blazed in the witch's gaze. "The child's mother is not mentioned in the story after I take her. It is not written that she will come for Rapunzel, but a prince will." She lifted her eyes to stare into my soul. "And so you must let it come to pass."

"Like hell I will." I snapped and my arms shot out but Mother Gothel didn't so much as flinch when I laid a hand on Ahri's chest. She didn't turn away or hold the baby tighter because she knew the child's lifeless body would make me stop and think before taking her away.

"Stay true to the story, Grimm, and she will live."

There it was. The truth that I knew deep down as soon as I saw the life fading from Ahri's face. The baby was dying. "How does kidnapping her save her life?"

Mother Gothel thrust out a single bony finger from where her hands were wrapped around the baby. She stepped back and my hand slipped from Ahri and fell limp at my side. I let her pull back the fabric that concealed the rift. I let her cross over because I had no answers and no other way to bring the dying child back to life. I wasn't a doctor and, it seemed, Ahri wasn't human because when Mother Gothel stepped into Storyland, blood returned to the baby's cheeks.

Hope lifted the weight that sat crushing the center of my ribcage as Ahri's nostrils expanded. Her pudgy cheeks twitched and her red lips parted as she released a gurgle.

Confident that I'd let her go now, Mother Gothel turned away from me. I reached through the rift and curled my fingers around her sleeve before she could take another step. She looked at my tight grasp on the fabric of her dress and then trailed her eyes up to my face.

"Let me go, Grimm."

"Why do you keep calling me that?"

The sickening smirk on her face twisted to a frown. "Now that you have come to the world that you have created, we recognize you. Those of us smart enough to see past your many faces, that is. A villain often has many faces, so it is easy to see in another. The veil is lifted, Grimm. Your mask is gone and we know who you are."

Blood turned to ice in my veins and I couldn't so much as blink. What in the fairy tale hell was she talking about? Goosebumps crawled up my arms and the sore muscles around my injured shoulder spasmed. I finally filled my lungs with a gulp of air and my mind cleared enough to connect the dots—or at least guess at the connection between the many names I'd been called lately. The wolf saw me as his author, but so did Mother Gothel.

Author. Grimm. Creator.

The *Author of All* as well as Sherlock's theory came to mind once again. One question remained, the same one that had plagued me after I'd killed the wolf. Why did these characters confuse me as this singular and time-transcending, all-powerful Author? I was never a writer—not of fiction, anyway. I wrote articles and reported crime for one purpose and one purpose only, to help keep innocent people safe.

"I'm not a villain," I said, breathless from the impact of her words. The suggestion behind her explanation left my stomach sour.

She lifted her chin and her dark braid fell over her shoulder like a thick rope. "Neither villain nor heroine. You are not a character, but a creator of both good and evil."

"No!" It was the only word I could think of as soon as 'evil' passed her lips. "You must be wrong because the wolf said I am a character. He said I wrote myself into Red Riding Hood's tale."

The ghost of a smirk flickered over her mouth. "I am not wrong. The wolf is not wrong. The Author has seen themselves in many stories, but is still first and foremost The Creator."

My grip loosened, but I did not let go while I searched the world behind her for understanding. Storyland was a vision of unrest as a bolt of lightning from Zeus or Thor or any other storm-wielding character struck the yellow road, shattering the brick into bits only inches away from Mother Gothel. The second time the sky lit up, the bolt landed on a figure in the background. I grimaced at the sight of the reincarnated Gingerbread Man meeting his death again. The jagged lightning split the body made of ginger cookies down the middle until he fell limp, crumbling to pieces over the destroyed brick.

"Release me before the storm kills us," Mother Gothel said. Her eyes fell to where my fingers grasped her dress and a frown wrinkled her chin. "Here, I am a sorceress and if you try to stop me, I will wield my power. There is only one way to change a story." Her dark eyes sparkled. "And if you so choose, give Mother Gothel—give *me*—the victory when you write it, not the prince."

I opened my mouth but nothing came out. Like the Little Mermaid, my voice was lost, at least temporarily.

The witch raised her eyebrows, and her lips curved into a wicked grin. "Goodbye Grimm. Or Perrault, whichever face you are wearing today." The names caused my heart to skip a beat, and when she turned, I let the fabric slip from my fingertips.

"Mari," I whispered as she disappeared behind the cloak of the red hood. "I'm Mari Fable Rowan…the *Coward*." My lungs deflated with a rough exhale and my shoulders sagged.

I couldn't bring myself to follow her into the wasteland of war. Not alone. Not in my condition. Even if I could tell the characters what to do, it would not save Ahri's life—not in the human world, anyway.

I closed my eyes as the hood's fabric shrouded the entire rift once again and Mother Gothel was out of sight. If these villains were right, could I do as Scarlet had suggested and twist the story to save Ahri? If I were the all-powerful Author, could I rewrite the baby's fate and bring her home? Or was she damned to exist in Storyland, forever?

My eyelids peeled open, and my lips parted. The bitter taste of truth lingered on my tongue, and I took a shuddering and cleansing breath. If nothing else, I had to rewrite Ahri's story the way I had saved my daughter—really myself—from the wolf all those years ago. Instead of using the powers of a magical hood, I put my faith in myself and banked on the belief of the characters who'd called me by their author's name.

This time I wouldn't use the hood or my gun to solve the problem, but a pen. I clung to the shred of hope that this insane plan could work, I just needed to find that pen… and a pad of sticky notes.

Chapter Eighteen

"Who will not change a raven for a dove?"

— William Shakespeare, A Midsummer Night's
Dream

On my way down the hill, I called Carlos and explained everything. The heartbreak in his strained voice gutted me and Scarlet's soft cries in the background sent me over the edge. Tears slipped down my cheeks as I told him about Ahri's lifeless body. My footsteps pounded the pavement with the same rhythm as my shuddering breaths. The tears were salty as they soaked my lips before I wiped them away with the back of my hand.

An occasional passerby double-glanced at me as I marched past other San Franciscans, brazen in my emotions. If I lived a normal life —the life I craved—I'd be crying over a breakup, a job loss, or a mountain of overwhelming laundry after a night of little sleep. Okay, I didn't *crave* any of those but at least I understood them. At least I'd know I was a woman dedicated to her life as a mom and to her career as a reporter. At least if I had an identity crisis forcing me to look at the darker parts of myself, it wouldn't involve villainy.

I listened to Carlos speak softly to Scarlet on the other line as I patiently waited for him to return to the phone. When he did, I promised him I would find a way to bring Ahri back alive—but it was a trial and error kind of idea.

Sirens echoed from somewhere in the city, sounding their desperate alarms and I was left to wonder which monster had slipped from Storyland. I'd yet to find Titania and convince her to return to Oberon which meant the king of the fairies may have come here to play tricks on the humans. If his jealousy had reached its breaking point, I wouldn't put it past him to throw around a few potions more dangerous than love. But Titania was a problem for another time—a rewritten story on another sticky note.

While my mind wandered, Carlos relayed the information to Scarlet in the gentlest tone possible.

Outside our condominium building, I climbed the staircase with the phone still pinned against my ear. Memories of the months before flashed through my mind from when the Snow Queen had been murdered here, pushed off the stairs to fall to her death on the concrete below. The torment my family and now Scarlet's family had to endure at the whims of fairy tale drama could all end if I sealed the rift. But first, Ahri needed to survive outside Storyland. I couldn't seal her inside and away from her family which meant the end of the stories' influence over the human world would have to wait.

On the other line, a momentary silence fell, and I assumed Carlos was busy comforting the mother of his child. Soft cries and sniffles broke through the quiet and my heart cracked.

At the top of the stairs, wind howled through the long outdoor hallway. I blinked away memories of Mr. Geppetto's daughter murdered on my doorstep at the hands of the wolf. The wolf that had turned from a human, anyway. Now I faced Storyland's wolf, a villain who apparently knew me better than I knew myself.

I wiped the evidence of sticky tears from my cheeks and sucked in a calming breath before telling Carlos the rest of my plan to return their daughter. It was the longest shot anyone had ever taken but if my experience instructing characters in Storyland had taught me anything; it was that I wielded power even without Red's magical hood. I wielded power all on my own and I needed to learn that power, to understand it and then use it to our advantage.

"I'll rewrite Rapunzel," I said as I pushed through the door. Wendy leaped off the couch and threw her arms around my waist while I kicked off my shoes and dipped to my knees to return the hug.

"Will that work to keep Ahri alive here?" Carlos asked in a low tone, likely to keep from further upsetting Scarlet.

After another sigh, I said, "I don't know. I'm sorry."

"Don't." He breathed. "Don't be sorry. Write it, but if she can't survive here just call me Pinocchio."

My brow knitted, and a headache sparked with a dull throb at my temples. "What? I thought you hated the memory of your time as Pinocchio."

"I don't care, Mari," he said, voice tight. He cleared his throat and continued. "I will become a character and live in Storyland if it means I can be with my daughter. Write me into it if you can, and Scarlet too. Call me as soon as you know anything new."

"I'll hurry."

"Don't," he demanded again. "If the villains are right and you have this power, then anything you write will determine our lives. Take your time and get it right. Even if you have to sleep on it. We'll be here resting while Scar recovers and then we'll be ready for whatever it takes to see Ahri again."

With that, the line went dead. Carlos, or Pinocchio, or maybe even *Carlo* again, was ready to risk his entire existence in order to reach his child… and Scarlet had been worried they weren't ready to be parents. In my messed-up opinion, they were already better parents than they could have ever imagined.

I swallowed the lump in my throat and finally let go of Wendy. She beamed at me as we pulled back and she ran little fingers through my hair. Evidence of my heartbreak was all but gone besides salt from the tears that had dried tightly on my skin. I mustered a small smile in return, mirroring the little reflections of myself in Wendy. Other than the determination and curiosity in her eyes and the frame of her face, we didn't share many similarities. The two front teeth were missing from her smile but she was the picture of perfection—or rather imperfection. Wonderful wild imperfection.

I tugged her into me for another hug when Kai emerged from the bedroom with Jack in his arms. "So, did you faint?" he asked.

Despite the elephant on my chest and the grief in my heart, I laughed at Kai's inference. I stood, releasing Wendy from my arms as I shot him a look of raised brows and then rolled my eyes.

"What?" he smirked and shifted Jack to his other arm. The oversized baby clapped and then reached for his mama. Kai swooped a stuffed crab toy into his hands to entertain him while we talked. "It's tough watching someone else give birth right? Spectators don't get all the extra endorphins that the laboring mom does."

"The 'spectators' are also not *laboring*," I said, emphasizing the word to drive home its meaning. "But I'll admit I got a little lightheaded."

As we moved to the couch, sinking into the soft worn cushions, I told him everything from the wolf's appearance outside the library to Zeus striking down the Gingerbread Man. Kai nodded along, bouncing a happy Jack on his leg.

"So," Kai started with a smirk, "you're basically Doctor Who?"

"If you mean that I've supposedly reincarnated or manifested as different authors throughout history, maybe. But I have no idea. It's too far-fetched for me to wrap my head around."

He cocked his head, and his hair fell to the side. "Is it though?"

I scoffed and tore my gaze from him as I scanned the mess of used dishes, a bottle, a breast pump borrowed from the hospital, books, and pens on the coffee table.

"Think about it, Mari. You're the only character who has twisted your own story. Even without the hood, you have superhero mind powers in Storyland." I shook my head, but he didn't stop. "And what about your blood? You touched the manuscript in the rift and it marked the pages."

At the mention of the crimson edits, I winced. I brushed my finger-tips over my temples, expecting a bolt of pain through my head as the image of myself bent over a handwritten copy of *The Wonderful Wizard of Oz* resurfaced. As if on cue, the headache surged, and I squeezed my eyes shut while the memory played through my mind's eye. In the memory, I sat at a little wooden desk, scribbling the words *The End* and then moved my hand to the bottom of the page where I signed it as L. Frank Baum in the same handwriting as I'd written today's notes.

What the hell? This had to be from a dream or a manifestation from my tired brain. My eyes popped open to Kai nodding at me.

"Maybe you're not...wrong," I said.

"My wife is a god of stories." He grinned cheekily.

I bumped my good shoulder against his and shook my head. "Not as cool as Buffy right?"

"Way cooler."

My gaze dropped from Kai to the baby in his lap. Chubby fingers reached for me and I gave his little hand a squeeze before scooting to the edge of the couch and swiping the block of sticky notes from the middle of the mess.

Wendy helped me clear clutter from the coffee table by carrying stacked dishes to the kitchen. She retrieved our worn copy of *Rapunzel* from the shelf that balanced our TV and delivered it to me. I moved stacks of books to the rug beneath the table, leaving only the imme-diate fairy tale within reach.

Finally, I peeled the sticky notes off one by one and arranged them in rows and columns. The top row was green, representing the original fairy tale while the column down on the far left was red for the new pieces I'd add. Below the right angle, I filled in the space with blue sticky notes where the original and the new version would come together to save the baby. I had a feeling I couldn't ignore the original entirely.

Kai shifted Jack to the floor who scooted around, dragging himself across the rug by using his hands to grip the shag carpet and then pull the rest of his body inches along. He looked like a pudgy worm, or perhaps a snail with the trail of shimmering frost his hands left behind on the rug.

Wendy plopped on the floor in front of Jack and pried a shard of ice from his hand just before he was about to take a bite out of the sharp edge. At Kai's request, she put little blue mittens over Jack's hands which frustrated him but helped the ice melt before it could form into another shard. It worked for now, but the more dexterity he developed the harder it would be to keep our son safe from himself.

I tore my eyes from my children, focusing instead on how to bring my best friend's child home. I flipped the copy of *Rapunzel* open and started scribbling each plot point from the original tale. Along the column, I added ideas of how I could write Ahri into our world.

Mother Gothel's magic is creating portals, and she escapes to the human world?

Rapunzel's hair leads down a skyscraper to the streets of San Francisco?

The witch's garden is a rooftop garden in the city and when Scarlet eats the Rampion, she turns into a human baby?

"Can I go that far back?" I muttered. "Can I change what has already happened?"

Kai hummed beside me as he looked over the notes and cross-referenced it with the website he'd pulled up about the history in the time of *Rapunzel*'s original inspiration. "But that hasn't happened yet in our world so maybe you can start there? Technically the father, Carlos, never made a deal with the witch. Scarlet was hungry, found out she was pregnant and then she staved off the cravings with sandwiches from the Girled Cheese and the best junk food San Francisco offers. Speaking of which." He flipped the website away and tapped a mobile food order app on the screen of his phone. "You need some fuel if you're going to use your goddess powers." He glanced at me with a wink before returning to scroll through the hundreds of restaurants available to order from.

Home life swirled around me while I sat glued to the couch cushions and with the pen in my hand. I crossed out ideas and cursed under my breath when I couldn't figure out how to give Rapunzel's parents more power in the story. The food arrived with a knock at the door and when Kai answered, the styrofoam containers filled the room with the smell of beans and cheese and salsa. Wendy argued about bedtime until Kai offered to read her a fifth story. While they read aloud from a chapter book, Jack wailed for attention.

I scooped him into my lap with a grunt and bounced him between scribbles. Even after I made a bottle and angled Jack so that he could drink while I wrote, he'd push the bottle away and complain with erratic cries as his frozen hands turned the milk to ice. More often than not, use of his magic made him upset, but not using his magic angered him as well. I tried to entertain him with a YouTube show of a woman singing and clapping along to popular children's songs. The Ms. Rachel episodes saved the day, distracting Jack from his frosty fingers long enough to let me finish an idea.

I filled in all the blue sticky notes where the two stories would weave together and then fetched a notebook from the stack under the table. Slowly, carefully, and with the same messy handwriting that I saw in the memory, I started creating a new version of *Rapunzel*. In my retelling, the child herself craved Rampion and Mother Gothel's deal was with Scarlet and Carlos to take the crying baby back to the human world and give her peace.

After the conclusion, I wrote *The End* and then moved the pen to the bottom of the page where I signed it with my name. I resisted the urge to add the title "Coward" after my name.

Nothing happened.

No call from Carlos that Mother Gothel had returned with a screaming child—a live, breathing version of Ahri even in the human world.

What had I expected? For the mountains to move at the behest of my scribbles? For the earth to shake after I signed my stupid name at the bottom of the page?

I had no idea what to expect, or think, or what to do next but Jack was snoring softly in my arms and the lull of Kai's voice reading from the other room had me sinking into the cushion. My eyelids grew heavy without my permission and I fought the exhaustion until I remembered Carlos's suggestion to sleep on it. Maybe I was missing a plot point, or I needed to rewrite it a few more times with careful edits. Maybe I needed rest before my brain worked to full capacity or my 'powers' revived.

I finally allowed my eyes to slide shut and the darkness to take over.

Chapter Nineteen

"Are you sure That we are awake? It seems to me That yet we sleep, we dream."

— William Shakespeare, A Midsummer Night's
Dream

O ver and over and over again I witnessed the Gingerbread Man's brutal murder. Many of his deaths came from the correct source, or the original tale's ending which involved a fox eating the Gingerbread Man a quarter at a time. Each sickening dinner, the fox grew quicker and quicker in his tricks and the Gingerbread Man's demise came suddenly and even more brutally.

When the story didn't play out correctly, lightning struck the poor cookie down at the whims of angry mythological gods. Other times he suffered stabbings by famous fictional warriors. The Gingerbread Man was beheaded by Mordred, poisoned by the Evil Queen, stepped on by the giant from *Jack and the Beanstalk*, shredded by *The Jungle Book's* Shere Khan, and finally—most disturbingly—devoured by the wolf.

Blood dripped from the wolf's glistening lips.

I woke with a gasp, my heart thundering and cold sweat soaking the front and back of my shirt. Goosebumps trailed my bare arms and neck and a shiver shook my entire body. The chill of the sweat had me reaching for a wrinkled blanket strewn over the back of the couch.

I clutched the fleece, cuddling the soft fabric of stars and moons against my chest like my life depended on it. Stuck in the nightmare, my mind replayed each death. Nausea surged from my stomach to my throat and I tasted bile at the same time I remembered the bloodstains on the fur around the wolf's mouth.

The Gingerbread Man was literally a living cookie, so who was bleeding from within the beast's gut? Red's blood. It was Red's blood, just as I had written it. In a time long ago and a land faraway, I sat down and penned the tragedy of the girl in the woods.

I knew for sure now. Sleep had cleared my head, and the puzzle formed a picture.

It wasn't a dream. It was a memory, as evident by the raging headache that plagued my temple and blurred my vision of the contemporary world around me.

I was the author who'd created the horror of *Little Red Riding Hood*. As clearly as I remembered the moment of conception when I spoke the words into existence, I couldn't recall why I'd spoken them. Why had I—an ancient storyteller—performed a story where an innocent young girl gets devoured? I shuddered and tugged the blanket into the dip at the bottom of my neck, nearly choking myself with the attempt at comfort.

Finally, in the darkness of the early morning, my eyes adjusted, and I scanned the surrounding area until I threw off the blanket and bolted to my feet.

"Where's Jack?" I whispered into the darkness and shuffled around the coffee table. Ripples of nausea rose in my belly to match the rhythm of throbbing in my head. I swallowed the pain and bit back a string of curses when my shin slammed into the corner of the wooden table.

Maybe I wasn't an all-powerful being but merely a clumsy lady with wild dreams. If only.

I stumbled past the kitchen and into the bedroom where Kai was curled asleep on the bed and Jack's bassinet was pulled within arm's reach. At the sound of my heavy footsteps, Kai stirred, sitting upright and blinking the blur of sleep away.

"Are you okay?" he asked as he raked his hand through his hair to pull it away from his eyes.

Thoughts of the repeated deaths haunted me. Even in the dim light of dawn, Kai could see the horror on my face. He reached out his arms and beckoned me to the bed. Like a child afraid of the dark, I crawled under the covers and let him wrap his arms around me while I told him every detail of my nightmare.

His warm breath tickled the back of my neck. "What's really bothering you?"

I blew out a breath as I considered the truth. "I think. No, I *know* that if the Gingerbread Man reincarnated that quickly then the wolf is back too."

"Then you'll shoot him again."

I shook my head. "It's not that simple. The Gingerbread Man's deaths were quicker each time. Eventually, the wolf will be faster than a bullet and stronger than I can fight off."

He tightened his hold on me and gently kissed the back of my head. "Good thing we're sealing the rift and he'll never be able to come back."

My throat tightened. "I created this, Kai." His silence was a question and an encouragement for me to continue but I struggled to find my voice again. I cleared my throat and steadied my breathing. "I remember." The words came out in a hoarse whisper. Again, he waited in quiet patience. As always, Kai not only believed me, he supported me. For now that support came in the strength of his comforting hold and the power of his silence. As dawn arrived, the sun brightened the room, peering through the slats in a sleepy faint glow. "I remember writing *Little Red Riding Hood*." I chewed at my lip and considered the memory, the surge of information that came with the headaches, and the unexplained control I'd wielded over Elizabeth Bennet, Juliet, Jane Eyre, and Puck. In Storyland, I spoke the power into existence. I'd even told the wolf what to do. But here, I was supposed to write what I wanted to occur, according to the villains. So why hadn't we heard from Carlos that Ahri was saved?

I sat up with a start, pulling away from my husband's hug, and twisted on the mattress to face him. The morning's arrival made it possible for me to see the tired lines that creased the corners of his eyes and the hollow beneath his cheekbones from stress-induced weight loss. He was as handsome as ever with his shaggy hair and the curve of his perpetual smirk but my heart ached at the hints of the worry, fear, and horror he'd endured. If only we could seal the rift and I could wipe my hands of this strange power. "Did Carlos call?" I finally asked.

"*Carlo*," Kai corrected with a sigh. "He's going by Carlo again. Or Pinocchio, if that's required."

"So he did call?"

Kai's bicep flexed as he ran his fingers through his hair again. A nervous tick that'd eventually render him bald if he tugged any harder. "Yes. The call woke Jack who was crying and woke me. You were dead to the world." *To* this *world.* Goosebumps popped up again, bringing with them the chill of sensitive skin. "I answered and since there was no news, I opted to let you rest. I told him you'd written the story and were sleeping. He seemed happy with that. He said you'd know why, whatever that means."

A joyless smile twisted my face. "I guess." *I have bad news. The sleep didn't give me answers for a new story.* "So there was no visit from Mother Gothel? I wrote it in a way that would force her to bring the baby back here and make a deal with the parents. I twisted it around but—" my voice caught on a lump in my throat and anger burned in my chest. Anger was always easier than disappointment so I welcomed the fire beneath my ribs and stoked the flame with heaving breaths and a grimace. "Why the hell didn't it work?" I'd found my voice now, and it came out full of vitriol and too loud.

Jack whimpered once, twice and then erupted into a battle cry that'd wake the entire building. The emotion in his screams only fueled me. Scarlet and Carlo should get to hear Ahri's cries. As tough as sleepless nights and raising a newborn were, it was better than knowing their baby was in the arms of a villain.

Kai kicked his legs around me and over the side of the bed and then scooped Jack into his arms, seething at our son's icy touch. Frost spread where Jack's thick fingers dug into his daddy's neck as Kai lifted him to see me over his shoulder. He patted Jack's back, but it only soothed him for a second.

Despite my son's desperate reach for me—the poor child hadn't been with his own mother enough lately—I stood and walked past them. If Jack missed me this much for the short time I'd been busy and away, how much pain was Ahri in since she'd been ripped from her mother's hold? How many days passed in Storyland while their baby developed and grew without them?

"Where are you going?" Kai asked, raising his voice just above Jack's angry wailing.

At the doorway, I turned and winced at the sight of our son's pinched red face and the shards of ice forming in his fists. "To the rift. To rewrite. To Storyland if I have to. I can't sit around and wait for the stupid story to fix itself. I have to keep trying to write it until Mother Gothel marches her grumpy butt back into Pioneer Park!" Kai's eyebrows lifted, accentuating the wrinkles of fatherhood on his forehead. He looked distinguished, curious, and incredibly sexy. I shoved thoughts of my husband away and forced a grim smile. "I'll be careful." I promised, before slipping from the bedroom and into the kitchen.

Right there in the middle of the tile floor stood my mini me staring back at me. Though we didn't look much alike, Wendy mirrored me with her mouth pursed in determination and her eyes narrowed with stubborn suspicion. She placed her hands on her hips as if she were the parent and I the child. "I'd like to go to the park too please," she said with all the sophistication in the world.

I matched her pursed lips and narrowed my gaze. "Okay, you can play while I write."

She shook her head, sending her messy hair flinging side-to-side. "I want to help." I resisted the urge to roll my eyes. After all, she was taking after me as she inserted herself into a situation that might serve to save another person. As obnoxious as her stubborn insistence was, I knew she only wanted to save people the same way I'd wanted to help in Storyland, and as an investigative reporter, and even as The Keeper of Stories.

My resolve withered at the ferocity in her voice. "Fine, you can help me think of revisions."

At that, she smiled and disappeared into her room, emerging only once she had located her fox backpack. She stuffed it full of juice boxes, peanut butter crackers, and granola bars and then marched across the living room to dig her shoes out of the pile by the front door.

Kai emerged from the bedroom with the baby in mittens. Jack munched on the fabric of his blue mittens, soaking the edge with his spit. His doughy cheeks bulged as he spotted me and smiled. I planted a kiss on his head where he'd rubbed the hair nearly bald.

After updating Kai on the plan to bring Wendy, I gathered my notebook, sticky notes, two pens, and my gun, before bidding goodbye with a promise to return as soon as we won back Rapunzel. The boys waved as the door swung shut. Well, Kai waved, and he held Jack's frozen fist into the air for a pretend wave.

THE WALK WAS refreshing and rigorous, and I refused to slow for Wendy's sake. Not that she needed it. Even on the steep hill, she kept up with my quickened pace. She didn't startle as blaring sirens blew past us on the street and she didn't slow when I explained the threat of the wolf at the rift. She didn't so much as flinch at my warnings.

"I'm serious, Wendy," I said between huffing breaths. The climb to the top of the hill was worse the morning after nightmarish sleep. "The wolf is terrifying. If we see him, you will run and if you can't run, you'll hide immediately and close your eyes so you don't have to watch me shoot him."

She nodded. "Deal. And I'll throw rocks."

"Wendy."

"What?" she looked up at me, eyes innocent and wide. "You've always told me you're never supposed to go anywhere alone."

I frowned. She wasn't wrong. We crested the concrete hill and followed the winding path into the park. Pioneer Park was almost entirely empty this early in the morning save for an occasional runner. The serious marathon trainers jogged by, some carrying Mace on their runners' belts and all engrossed in their pacing and whatever they listened to on their headphones and earbuds.

The lamp posts still glowed with a dim yellow since the sun hadn't quite reached high enough in the sky yet. The park was dark to match both my mood and the stories the other versions of myself had written.

We sat on a double-sided bench by the playground. One seating area faced the play structure where parents could take a rest as they watched their children get rid of excess energy. On the other side, we had a view of the center of the park where we could see the scrap of the hood's fabric billowing in the gentle breeze that curled through the surrounding trees.

I balanced the notebook on my lap and clicked open a pen as Wendy scooted closer to me. "Read it aloud," she said.

I glanced down at her, one eyebrow arched. "You know how to read."

She shrugged. "But it's easier if you read it aloud."

Again, she wasn't wrong. Plus, it matched my former self, the part of my alternate past that had been coming back in bits and pieces. A long time ago I'd been an oral storyteller, and recently the same power worked in Storyland.

I may as well try both. So I began the rewrite and the storytelling at the same time, all while monitoring the rift. At times, I expected the wolf to burst through, snarling and bloodthirsty as he ripped past the red veil. Though I waited with bated breath for the villain of my story —Red's story—I hoped for *Rapunzel's* villain. I hoped Mother Gothel would peel back the blood-red fabric and offer us a bundled baby at the beck and call of my written words.

I wrote a version where Rapunzel wielded magic more powerful than Mother Gothel's and the witch returned her to our world to keep the threat at bay.

Nothing happened.

I wrote a version with no villain as per Wendy's suggestion. In this retelling, Mother Gothel was a good witch who granted Rapunzel a life in the human world.

Nothing happened.

I wrote a version that aged Rapunzel rapidly and gave her the agency to wish upon a star to find her parents. Both of us held our breaths and stared unblinking at the rift in case a toddler-sized Ahri waddled up to the rift and climbed over the edge.

Nothing happened.

The sun reached its peak in the sky, shining through the treetops and casting scattered beams across the park's concrete center. More San Francisco locals came and went, marching by the rift without notice. Joggers and dog-walkers and people on their lunch breaks passed by as the electronic watch on my wrist displayed the minutes and hours that were wasted away while I accomplished exactly nothing.

I wrote and rewrote, scribbling in the margins, crossing out old ideas, adding new plot points, and twisting *Rapunzel's* characters in as many retellings as I could imagine until the entire notebook was filled to the brim. The words spilled over onto every sticky note I'd brought with me and when both sides of those were covered in ideas; I dropped the pen.

It rolled off the notebook and fell to the bench where it slipped between the slats and clattered to the concrete beneath us. Wendy peered through the crack and then looked up at me.

I hung my head, defeated by the story, by the edits and revisions, by the mistake I'd made. Something was wrong. Mother Gothel and the wolf must have been wrong about me. I couldn't bring forth a new story with some unexplained Author-of-All power. "I'm not a writer," I said, weak in my frustration. I scooted back and balanced my elbows on my knees before letting my head drop into my hands.

Between my fingers I saw Wendy point at the overwritten lines of the notebook. "But you wrote a lot." She cocked her head to read the scribbles. "It's so much I can't even see the words."

I arched my neck, keeping my chin perched in the center of my right palm and gestured my three fingers at the rift. "It doesn't matter. I'm not a writer so it isn't working."

We sat in silence for too long. It was a good thing Wendy thought to pack snacks in her fuzzy fox backpack because time slipped away. I couldn't bear to wonder how frustrated and distraught Carlo and Scarlet felt. Jack needed me at home. Ahri needed me in Storyland. Hell, *all* of Storyland needed me, including the poor Gingerbread Man, yet here I sat.

A family on an early evening walk passed by. The father carried a girl about Wendy's age on his shoulders while the mother pushed a stroller with twin babies. They laughed and talked and enjoyed the park's fresh air as they walked right next to the rift. I tensed and Wendy glanced at me.

"What?" she asked, looking between me and the rift. "Is the wolf going to get them?"

"I don't know," I admitted. "But I suppose I should warn people about this park, huh?" I scanned Pioneer Park which was devoid of life now. The family had disappeared down an exit path, leaving us alone to stare at the rift.

Would the wolf attack innocent passersby? He had hunted only me before but I couldn't predict what he might do now. *Little Red Riding Hood* was written—I'd written it—that way. He devoured the grandma so that he could devour the girl. Why had I created such an awful story? And why did this weird past version of myself try to do it again with *The Little Cloak Girl*? One ended in tragedy, much like the articles I wrote to warn the people of San Francisco about local murders. The other didn't end at all.

Wendy dug out a juice box from her backpack and put it on the notebook in my lap. "You don't look good."

I forced air through my nose in an odd, joyless laugh. "Gee thanks Kiddo."

She shrugged, pulled out an apple juice for herself, stabbed the straw through the box, and started sipping. Her legs swung back and forth beneath the bench. "Are you going to tell people to stay away from the park on the news?"

I tore my gaze from the rift and looked down at her. "You mean like through my job's website?"

Her bony shoulders lifted and fell in another shrug. "Yeah, you're a reporter so you can report the bad guys. Right?"

"Right..." my voice trailed. My mind swirled with the suggestion. *I'm a reporter*. I wasn't a writer, never would be. But I was a dang good reporter. My gaze narrowed on the fluttering fabric at the rift. On the other side, the manuscript was there with my blood on the countless pages of recorded oral stories, plays, poetry, and more. What had the Wizard of Oz said about Sherlock's theory? I scraped my brain to remember the details. According to the genius detective, the creator of all the tales was sometimes a poet and other times a playwright, not always a writer or novelist. Could the iterations of the all-powerful Author manifest with unique talents?

What about a reporter? What if I couldn't simply write Rapunzel's story in order to change Ahri's fate? What if I needed to play to my specific talents and report the danger lurking in Pioneer Park? I could warn the city about an old woman stealing babies from the hospital. First, I wanted to confirm the theory with a little history. There was no reason to waste more time by writing an article and convincing my boss at Bay Side Media to publish it if it wouldn't even work to save Ahri...or seal the rift.

I needed to get my hands on *The Author of All* and learn the details of this wild reincarnation theory. What I needed was to pay the library another visit.

"Mommy?"

The threads that had woven theories in my brain unraveled at the interruption. I blinked and gave my daughter my full focus. "Yes, Wendy?"

"You don't look so bad anymore." She beamed, swinging her legs with even more energy. "I knew the juice would help. It always helps me."

I picked up the juice box and pushed the straw through the foil opening before taking a sip of the refreshing apple flavor. "How does a break at the library sound?"

Wendy tilted her head and squinted, staring at nothing before she met my gaze. "Can we get grilled cheese first?"

I offered her my good hand for a shake. When she accepted, we sealed the deal and my spirits lifted—if only slightly. Maybe today wasn't such a failure after all.

Chapter Twenty

"You had the power all along, my dear."

— L. Frank Baum, The Wonderful Wizard of Oz

I frowned at the amniotic fluid stain on the carpet underneath my favorite library table. When Wendy returned with a stack of *Nancy Drew* novels and saved the corner table, I ventured down the aisle and located *The Author of All* from the shelf. The nearly abandoned row of books was covered in a blanket of dust. My finger traced the tome's spine until I slid it halfway out of the tightly packed shelf.

The green hardcover was too wide to carry with my three fingers so I ignored the pain in my right shoulder and lifted my arm to grab the book with my good hand. Back at the table, I carefully turned the thick pages as I quickly scanned the text.

Apparently, this book had been written by a historian. Someone like Kai who had recognized that studying the past could help predict the future. And as much as I appreciated that, neither my past self nor the future version of Mari was tasked with saving someone else's daughter from a war and a witch. It was the present moment that I hoped the information in this book could help me clarify.

I poured over the pages, curious about every similarity identified between classic literature, ancient stories, and fairy tales. As much as I wanted to stop and study all the information, I was skimming for patterns. In certain time periods, the similarities appeared only in poetry. Later on, the historian identified unique phrases used in all 1800s novels. My finger landed on a list of recorded fairy tales from Charles Perrault, the Brothers Grimm, and Hans Christian Andersen. I slowed my reading over the following paragraph.

Though one hundred years existed between these writers, there is undeniable proof that the same hand penned the unique phrases. The language and voice matches in a way that even professional writers today can not mimic that closely. It remains to be explained how The Writer lived for as long as they did.

My eyes fell to the footnote at the bottom of the page that referenced the list of unique phrases at the back of the book. The phrases, language, and author voice were identified across all the stories, poetry, plays, and fairy tales studied. I flipped to the front of the book and checked for a publishing house but it appeared the historian had self-published the study, likely because they'd been marked as someone who'd lost their marbles.

Considering this, I pulled my gaze from the text and fixed my eyes on the library's back wall. Wendy read and hummed happily in the same tone as her father's made-up songs. I sank against the hardback of the chair and pulled the tome into my lap because it seemed we'd settled in for an evening of reading. The rough and thick elastic attached to my hidden holster dug into the soft flesh of my stomach but I didn't dare leave the weapon at home knowing the wolf would be back.

I ignored the uncomfortable holster and thumbed to the back of the book, pausing at the last section just before the collection of phrases and footnote references. *The Divine Author.* The chapter's title caused a skip in the beat of my heart. I definitely wasn't a divine being. I wasn't even a writer.

According to the historian, the creator of all the literature from ancient to classic had the divine power to transcend time and place, and possess artists across centuries. The historian explained how the 'Divine Author of All' or DAA as they called *her*, bouncing between both titles and the term 'goddess of myth, folktale, and chronicle,' exhibited specific *focuses* during specific time periods. The belief fit with Sherlock's theory that the singular Author sometimes only wrote novels and other times became a poet.

It also matched my theory.

Storyteller in Storyland. Writer, poet, playwright in the past. Reporter in the present?

With this wild confirmation of my ridiculous idea, I felt justified in the time it would take to create an official article and report on *Rapunzel*—or rather, the retelling of it for Ahri's sake. If nothing else, it was worth a try. Anything was worth a try to get my best friend's baby back home.

I slapped the book shut and straightened, scooting to the edge of the seat. I stood and announced to Wendy that it was time to borrow the books so we could go home. There, I'd have my laptop and a historian husband to back up my plan. I had a boss to email and an article to write.

After we checked out the rentals with the librarian, Wendy's stack of *Nancy Drew* mysteries and my single *Author of All* book, we stuffed the books into Wendy's fox backpack and I threw it over my good shoulder. Hanging from one strap, it bounced against my back as we stepped outside and hurried down the concrete steps.

On the streets, San Francisco was buzzing. Tourists, students from the local college, couples, partiers, and late-evening workers filled the sidewalk. It was nothing I wasn't used to but tonight felt different. Tonight I felt eyes on us.

I stopped in the shadow of a shop's overhang and scanned the street for yellow eyes. The wolf was likely healed now, having returned whole from Storyland. Squealing sirens drowned any chance of hearing his rough growls or the scrape of his claws against concrete. My pulse sped up with every second that I couldn't spot him. I'd feel so much safer and more confident if I could pinpoint his location and get Wendy away from him. Before, I'd taken comfort in the thought that he was only after me but after what I'd witnessed with the Gingerbread Man's repeated deaths, I couldn't be sure that innocents in the way—Wendy like the Gingerbread Man—wouldn't suffer the wrath of a villain on the hunt.

I reached for Wendy's hand and gently tugged her closer to me. Cars zipped by, honking at one another and large groups of rowdy people trampled past us. None of the big city threats were more than I could handle. Even the wolf himself hadn't bested me—not yet, but none of those thoughts truly calmed me. I felt for the hard frame of the gun in my holster. The bullets had kept him at bay before but I had no doubt he'd be faster now as he learned and evolved from each experience with me.

As we passed an alley, my ears pricked to the sound of his presence. The bellowing growl bounced off the narrow walls between restaurants. I spotted two glowing eyes emerging from the shadow behind a dumpster. His massive paw smashed a styrofoam container that had fallen from the overfilled trash and a street light shined off of the wetness slicked over his jagged canines.

I yanked Wendy along and nearly ran to the crosswalk where I buried us in the middle of a crowd, hoping to throw him off our trail long enough to get Wendy home. Then, I could deal with the wolf alone and with a full round of bullets.

We weaved through slower pedestrians as we followed a crosswalk onto Main Street. Still several blocks away, I picked up the pace again and encouraged Wendy to match it. Though her legs were short, soccer practice kept her in better shape than me.

"Is there a bad guy following us?" she asked, shouting above the noise of engines and footsteps. I glanced down at her and answered with a quick nod. No fear manifested in her eyes, only determination.

The closer we came to safety, the more my limbs felt like jello as relief flooded me. Once our condominium building came into view, I breathed even easier, confident now that I'd get Wendy home before the wolf attacked.

Unfortunately, the confidence didn't last when we found ourselves without the cover of a crowd. This side of Main Street was quieter with only an occasional passerby, and in the alley that led us to the parking lot and staircase at the back of the building, we were alone. Or so I'd hoped.

At the scratchy and grating sound of claws scraping concrete, adrenaline sent my emotions through whiplash as my heart rate climbed again. A snarl rumbled from the shadow of the alley. I pulled Wendy in front of me and told her to run up the staircase.

"Don't stop until you get into the house and lock the door."

"I can help!"

I shook my head, firm in my decision and furrowed my brows with a look of intensity until her little shoulders dropped and she relented. As she turned, she mumbled, "I can help."

I let her argumentative comment slide and watched her reach our floor before I spun and scanned the shroud of darkness created by the tall building next door. At the first sign of movement, I had my hand on my gun. Light flooded the alley for a moment as a car on Main Street sped past. Still, the wolf was nowhere to be seen.

Instead, a growl rattled my bones, closer than the alley and from the parking lot to my left. The parking lot led directly to the staircase for ease of tenant access and the wolf had likely chosen the lot so he could hide behind cars. To him they were nothing but thick obstacles that blocked him from a bullet, or so I guessed considering he had no qualms about charging me in plain sight before.

"You can't eat me if you don't come out of hiding," I said, hoping to bait him into view. My voice bounced back at me from the crowded parking lot. Low overhangs covered the lot to protect the vehicles from the elements, but tonight they only made the parking lot look cramped. Several large SUVs provided plenty of cover for the wolf so I took to scanning the ground for the movement of his shadow.

"It is you who should hide, Author," he said. His voice was a mix of unsettling purrs and gnashing teeth.

"I am not an author," I said since it was the only thing I could think of.

A shadow shifted beneath the jeep parked closest to the sidewalk. He was getting ready to pounce, and he'd gotten there thanks to the darkness provided by the overhang. If I couldn't see him before he attacked, I couldn't shoot him.

"Ebenezer Scrooge," I breathed. The hot air coiled into a steamy puff and then dissipated into the night.

Just as I had suspected, the wolf had evolved the same way the clever fox had in *The Gingerbread Man*. The experience he shared with me was an opportunity to survive the second time. I felt for the cold steel of the pistol's handle and flicked off the safety. Slowly, I side-stepped onto the staircase until I was positioned above the height of the car.

"Whatever you have manifested as in this world now is of no concern to me. You are *my* author and you always will be," he grumbled, clearly irritated that I'd suggested he was wrong. "You are my only desire."

I took another higher step and aimed my gun at where the shadow was cast on the ground to the side of the jeep. "Gee, I'd be flattered if I'd written this as a romance. Too bad the old author version of me didn't have the foresight to spin the tale of a shifter into a romance. Move over Twilight, there's a new werewolf love triangle. Though I have to spoil the ending for you, I'd choose Kai..." The words spewed out of me, a sign that my nerves had reached their breaking point and my brain had shifted to pure sarcasm.

Finally and brazenly, the wolf stalked out from behind the jeep. Ratty fur hung over thick shoulders that spiked above the top of his head with every step. His head hung low enough for his red tongue to graze the ground but instead of licking the gum off the sidewalk he drew it over his mouth, slick and shiny as it followed the dips and peaks of his sharp teeth.

It took entirely too long for me to shift my arms to a slight right for better aim and then to put a bullet in the wolf's skull.

He didn't care.

I pulled the trigger, firing in the same spot between his eyes for a second time. It should have killed him, or at least slowed his ominous march toward me, but the two well-aimed shots didn't phase him in the least.

Claws dragged against the concrete and I grit my teeth as I shot him again and again and again. The bullets disfigured his face enough to leave a gaping hole where his brow had been. Yellow eyes were nothing but husks of black as blood seeped from the hole and yet, he only came closer.

Inches away from the staircase now, he could leap with little effort, opening his jaw to devour me in a single bound. The gun clicked, clicked, clicked as I slammed the trigger helplessly. I cursed at the useless weapon, my voice quivering. I'd surpassed sarcasm as guttural fear gripped my tongue and death was only a breath away. My only chance at survival was escape.

I whipped around and my heels slammed against the next step, and then the next, and the next until bone shattering claws dug into the muscles between my shoulder blades and my body hit the staircase.

Humid breath heated my back and his saliva dripped onto the nodule of my spine at the base of my neck.

"Mari!" A shrill voice split the night.

The hot breath vanished but the wolf's paw grew heavier against my shoulder blades as he pushed me harder into the steps. My entire body should have ached but adrenaline masked all pain and I grabbed onto the step before me to pull myself from under his hold.

"Little Cloak Girl," the wolf said. I craned my neck to see the silhouette of a woman at the top of the staircase. Her thick curls created waves in the shadow of her frame. "Have you come to ruin Red's story again?"

My heart sputtered. *We were right.* Kai and I had been bloody right about the stupid theory. Scarlet was finally confirmed as the same Little Cloak Girl who'd wandered Storyland. There was no way the wolf would recognize her otherwise.

"What are you doing?" I breathed, raspy as I stared at her from beneath my furrowed brow. I had wanted no casualties and by the looks of it, Scarlet—a mother who had just given birth and lost her baby—had come to a wolf fight with nothing but her bare hands.

"Wendy said she wanted to help, so sending me out here is how she helped," she said. "Plus, you must not die."

The wolf laughed. "You will both die now. Little Red and the Little Cloak Girl who replaced her. All the better to eat you with, Red. A character and a creator." He huffed in what sounded like a second laugh. "All the better since I do not have a taste for creatures of this world. Lost girls from my neck of the woods are far more filling."

The weight of his paw lifted and the tips of his sharp claws released from where they'd sliced my shirt and buried into my flesh. Now the tiny holes were open wounds that stung when the salty San Francisco breeze rippled over my back.

He leaped clean over me and landed on the steps above, shaking the entire staircase with his massive body. He'd abandoned me—*me*, the object of his desire, the center of his story for Scarlet. And he wasn't confused like the other characters in Storyland because he knew exactly who we both were.

"Scar!" I squealed. I pushed to my knees, straightening as quickly as my shaking body would allow. My eyes adjusted to the dim light of the staircase and it was then I saw the blood red hood draped over Scarlet's shoulders. It was then I understood the scene before me.

It was then I knew her plan.

The wolf lunged for her, launching off of his hind legs and expanding his huge jaws to come down from above and swallow her from the head first. Scarlet yanked the hood over her head and something shiny flashed from within her fist before she dropped into a huddle and allowed him to eat her whole. His jaws snapped shut and my heart slammed into my stomach.

She was gone, eaten, and the wolf would turn to me next.

The silence in the seconds that passed sucked the oxygen from my lungs. It wasn't until the tip of a shiny blade thrust out of the wolf's back that I breathed again. Scarlet dragged the knife in a zigzag between every nodule of his arched spine until he split open and she was freed.

The wolf's two halves split like the Gingerbread Man but instead of crumbling into a pile of cookie dust, the monster faded. When he disappeared to Storyland ready to reincarnate, I could see the huddled figure in red more clearly. Scarlet sat curled within herself on the next landing above. She flicked back the hood and blew out a breath as she met my gaze.

"I opted to cut from the front," I said, seething as another gust of wind stung my back with salty air. Though it was a joke, I didn't smile, and neither did she. "You took the hood," I continued in observation of the garment that had saved her life.

"I took the hood," she said.

My voice dropped to a whisper. "How could you? How big is the rift now that you—"

"Mari!" She snapped, looking up at me through long lashes. Her head was hanging, chin tilted down and curls framed her face. Cold, hard determination dimmed her eyes and the angles of her cheekbones cast shadows on her fair skin. She looked as she had all those years ago when I'd first met The Keeper of Stories. "Listen to me. I'll do whatever it takes to get to my daughter."

"But—"

"No," she interrupted me again. "You did the same. You took the hood and now it's my turn to be a strong mother. I decided to take the hood when I remembered everything."

I didn't respond. I couldn't if I'd wanted to. I couldn't move much less speak or even blink as I waited for her explanation.

"Carlo told me what you'd learned about...*yourself*," she said, raising her chin as her voice lowered. "When I heard the concept again, I remembered what I'd once believed. Mari, I didn't wander into Storyland. I left it. And it wasn't to find my parents. I left to find you."

"What?"

"I was neither a hero nor a villain. I was a girl in a story without an ending. The lack of character motivation gave me clarity while all the others were single-minded. I could see the hand of my creator so I set out to find her and beg for her to finish the tale." I shook my head, as if the simple action could wholly reject this insanity. "Finish the fairy tale, Mari. Write me back into Storyland with my daughter. The Little Cloak Girl grows up to be the mother of a child named Rapunzel."

Tears filled my eyes faster than a wave crashing against the shore.

They spilled over my cheeks, hot and sticky. "I'll bring her back here…" my voice died at the shake of Scarlet's head.

"She's a character just like I am supposed to be."

"You're my best friend. You're Wendy's aunt!" I cried between shuddering breaths. "You can't leave."

Scarlet's eyes swam with a sadness that mirrored mine but behind the blurring tears—tears she easily blinked away—resolve was fixed within her gaze. "Please. You have fought this part of yourself for too long." The ghost of a wry smile flickered over her lips. "Why do you think the Brothers Grimm annoyed you so much? They were a manifestation of *you*."

"Oh, hell no." I threw up my hands in surrender though I knew she wasn't wrong. It made sense. Once I'd confronted the Grimm gods about their existence, they'd ceased to exist. They were figments of my imagination, compartments of knowledge stored away of identities once claimed and lives long passed. They were the parts of my brain that knew what'd I'd blocked out—what trauma and fear and death had taken from my memory. But just like the stories, I'd reincarnated and evolved with ghosts of my past selves haunting my every step.

Scarlet allowed me a moment to process, and when I met her gaze again she smiled. "Oh, hell yes."

My eyes slid shut as overwhelm made me woozy.

All at once, I saw my future, and it was plain. My future would become what I'd always desired. Mortality, mountains of laundry, and busy days at the office would become my biggest stressors, and as much as I relished the daydream, the days ahead were lonely without the woman I'd grown to love as family.

Scarlet straightened and drifted down the steps, closing the distance between us. She stretched out her arm and offered me her hand.

When I accepted it, we both knew I would fulfill her wish. I was The Creator, The Writer, The Poet, The Divine Author of All and already my mind buzzed with ideas to reunite Scarlet's little family, seal the rift, and stop this fairy tale hell once and for all.

Chapter Twenty-One

"A good moral, my lord: it is not enough to speak, but to speak true."

— William Shakespeare, A Midsummer Night's
Dream

The next day I found focus at the place I least expected. The white noise of the office's buzz helped me study both *Little Red Riding Hood* and the tale that had stolen Red's thunder. Behind me someone cursed at the broken printer, coworkers gossiped in muted conversations, and the espresso machine hummed with a soothing grind. It had been a long time since I'd sat hunched over my desk in a cubicle at Bay Side Media and I was enjoying every second of it.

I'd already spent the entire morning at my laptop with Scarlet standing over my shoulder. Half of the time she stooped over me with her arms crossed and her pickle breath breathing down my neck. Despite the unpleasant smell of pickles, I relished every second of her hovering because I knew this was the last time she'd ever annoy me. I was writing her out of my life—or rather, reporting on a story that'd seal her into Storyland. Forever.

My heart ached, but I was eager to reunite her with her daughter, and of course I added Carlo into the tale as well. In order to bring the three of them together, rid our world of the wolf and the rift, and keep the original message of the other fairy tales, I had to combine *Rapunzel, The Little Cloak Girl,* and *Little Red Riding Hood.* It was a mountainous challenge, but I'd written dozens of tough articles before.

Scarlet's hair tickled my shoulder as she leaned over me and scanned the computer screen. She pointed at the line where I'd typed up bullet points about the wolf. "You can't get rid of the wolf until he eats someone. Not if you want to keep *Little Red Riding Hood* as close to the original as possible."

"I'm aware," I grumbled. "What do you propose? He eats you?"

She straightened and crossed her arms over her chest. "Yes, exactly."

"Scar—"

"Mari. Stop waffling around and get to the meat of the story. There is no way to make everything happy ever after."

"What about the rift? I was thinking I can add a secondary world into the story and include that the portal between the two worlds heals itself."

She tugged at a curl and shook her head. "No. Simplify, Mari. Fairy tales are basic, straightforward stories that teach a lesson. You know what Red's story is supposed to be about."

I frowned and my stomach churned, sloshing around that second cup of coffee I regretted having. "Red's story was a warning," I said with a sigh.

"Bingo! And?" She waved me on.

"And that warning has taught people all across the world and throughout history how to stay safe."

"Just like...?" She prodded.

"Just like a reporter does. I've got it, okay?" I swatted her waving hand away and pointed for her to leave the cubicle. She didn't move. "I can't work like this, Scar."

She rolled her eyes. "As you wish." But the two steps she took back and the way she leaned on the cubicle wall wasn't what I wished.

I closed my eyes and tried to think of a way to thread the wolf into the tale. "What if the wolf tracks you through the portal?" I asked. I spun in the rolling chair to face Scarlet.

She shot me a thumbs down and blew raspberries with her tongue pinched between her lips. "The wolf has to *eat* someone."

"Right," I said as I grimaced and turned back to the computer. "How about this? The wolf's mouth becomes the portal and when he devours you, you return to Storyland."

"Good," she said, "now you're getting it. Just make sure you edit that out when you republish the article so that the rift no longer exists."

I muttered a retort about her bossiness and then swallowed my emotions. I was going to miss the blunt way she spoke along with all her colloquialisms and odd behaviors. Who was going to eat all our pickles? Who was going to drive me insane at work? Our children were meant to grow up together and become the best of friends.

When I sat too long without typing, Scarlet tapped her foot. Finally, I shoved the painful thoughts away and threw myself into the post. I was in a state of intense concentration, pouring over the differences between Red's story and *The Little Cloak Girl* as well as the other fairy tales when Scarlet finally walked away. Her voice drifted from the water cooler next to our boss's office.

"I won't be returning," she said to one of our coworkers.

Tears welled in my eyes when I realized she was saying her good-byes and officially quitting the job she'd worked so hard to get. Deep down, I knew she wasn't sad. I knew Scarlet was ready for happily ever after as a mom and a queen after she grew out of her cloak.

When Scarlet entered the boss's office and her voice faded out of earshot, I forced my focus on the task ahead of me. I needed to get the correct structure of the old-fashioned tales and weave the story into an article. While I wasn't technically back to work from my extended maternity leave, I'd been given my boss's approval to publish a reporter's post on Bay Side Media's "Local Living" blog. And later—once I returned to investigative journalism in an official capacity—I could expand on the post and turn it into an official article.

So I sat slumped in the desk chair and read and wrote and read and wrote until my eyes stung from staring at the screen and my fingers ached. Worst of all, my head pounded from dehydration as I cried softly on and off throughout the day. As I studied, the memories came back…memories of lives past lived. Of *my* lives and the reasons I'd created the stories that I did.

It was amazing what you could remember once you acknowledged a past your brain wanted to protect you from. It wasn't exactly traumatic being a time-transcendent storyteller, but the messages and themes I had to write were.

Last night we fought the wolf and won. Barely. Next time, we wouldn't be so lucky and I knew why. I'd written *Little Red Riding Hood* with purpose. Fairy tales, classic literature, even poetry and plays weren't simply intended for entertainment. Each one had a message, a lesson, a moral.

Scarlet's shadow cast over me as she stepped into the cubicle. "I know you'll miss me, Mari, but I can't stand to be away from my baby any longer."

I nodded. "I know, I'm hurrying. I just want to get this right for you and for Ahri and Carlo, and since we agree I shouldn't mess with the original purpose of *Little Red Riding Hood*, it's tricky." My voice quivered and a lump in my throat stopped me from explaining further. Another round of stinging tears flooded my eyes, blurring my vision so much that when I looked at Scarlet, she was swimming. Never had I cried so much in one day. Okay, maybe I'd gotten pretty close during the first trimesters of my pregnancies and also the day Wendy was born and then taken from me.

"Mari." She rested her hand on my shoulder and tilted her head. "I know you're going to miss me—" She quieted when I shook my head.

"I *will* miss you, but that's not the only reason I can't stop crying." Her brow knitted, and she shifted to take a seat on the desk next to my computer. I had her full attention now, but I didn't know if I was ready to put my feelings into words. After a moment, I cleared my throat and sucked in a breath. "It broke me, Scar, writing *Little Red Riding Hood* broke me."

Concern filled her emerald eyes. "But it wasn't the first tragic ending you created and it wouldn't be the last."

I nodded. "I know, and I knew I *had* to create Red's story because of the message. *Little Red Riding Hood*'s demise has served as a warning to millions of readers that the world is dangerous."

"And it teaches that people shouldn't go out alone."

"Also, the lesson that one must be careful when trusting strangers," I added, continuing the list as my tears temporarily dried. It felt good to talk about this and put into words what had been nagging at me, but it wasn't long before emotion welled again, blurring my vision and straining my voice. "That's my point. It was a crucial story full of purpose so it had to be written. Still, I hated that I wrote that Red got eaten by the wolf." I recalled the rest of the memories. "So I created dozens of other versions. When I called myself Perrault, I wrote the tragedy and years later I went by the Grimm name and rewrote the ending with Red and Grandma rescued by the huntsman. But it didn't matter." My throat tightened. "The original version was written, and it was the most important one. Not every story has a happily ever after, just like you said, but I was haunted by Red so I sat down one day and created *The Little Cloak Girl* as a final and happy version of Red's tale. I never finished it because I knew the real ending it needed. *Little Red Riding Hood* never should have been changed."

Silence fell between us as Scarlet absorbed the information. The office's white noise settled my pounding pulse but when her eyes widened into massive green saucers, it sped up again. "Was that why I was able to cross over into the other stories when none of the other characters could?"

I nodded. "I think so. It's also why the Wizard of Oz thought you were from the human world. Since no one else had ever passed the barrier of their own story before, you didn't seem like a character. None of the other stories were unfinished and because of their endings they were sealed while you wandered. And I'm pretty sure you had the power to wander right out of Storyland through a portal you'd created with your unwavering belief. You never gave up hope that your parents would find you, but it didn't stop you from looking for them. And for me, I guess."

Her eyes sparkled, and I swore a smile even graced her lips. I recognized the look of recalling precious memories. "That's right! I walked all over Storyland and gathered all the other characters' powers. Is that how the hood got empowered too?"

With another nod and pursed lips, I confirmed her speculation. "I believe so. Everything you learned and believed empowered you—all of you. And since the cloak was the title of your tale, the power went into it."

"Oh my goodness, it finally makes sense why you couldn't create portals!"

I shrugged. "Yeah, I was always envious of that. Saves a lot of energy and gas money."

With a laugh she said, "I guess you have to be a character in an unfinished story to jump around." After a moment, she fell silent and her long lashes dipped as she squeezed her eyes shut. "I can see it. I can see Storyland."

I reached for her hands in her lap and gave them a squeeze. "It's time to go back." When her eyes popped open again, she scooted off the desk and straightened. I pushed the rolling chair back and stood, throwing my arms around her.

Our hug reminded me of the wobbly and strange passage of time in Storyland. I had no idea how long we were wrapped in each other's arms but it wasn't long enough. When she pulled back, I tightened my hold on her until it squeezed the tears out of both of us.

Finally, I found my voice. "Are you ready?"

A laugh bubbled out of her as we released one another. "To die? Definitely not. But I'm ready to go home to Ahri."

Chapter Twenty-Two

"..fairies of Grimm and Andersen have brought more happiness to childish hearts than all other human creations. Yet.."

— L. Frank Baum, The Wonderful Wizard of Oz

The rift was no longer a scrap of fabric billowing in the wind. Without the hood, the rip between worlds looked more like an optical illusion. If you squinted at it just right, you could see straight into Storyland where *Wuthering Heights* butted up to the English countryside of *Pride and Prejudice*. But if you didn't stand in the perfect spot, the rift was impossible to see. Not to mention the dark of night that helped shroud it.

As soon as I pressed the button to publish the post, we knew the rift would vanish once it transported into the wolf's mouth. But first, we had to take a picture together.

Every single one of us gathered in front of the colorful play structure as Kai readied my phone to take a self-timed photo and then balanced it on the bench. Our beloved found family posed in front of the playground holding tense smiles on our faces. Carlo circled his arms around Scarlet's middle and Wendy sat on the ground in front, holding Jack in her lap while Kai and I mirrored the other couple. Everybody said "cheese" as the phone's light blinked and then paused, signaling that the photo had been taken.

"This will be the only photo of us all together," I said as I walked back to the bench with Scarlet at my heels. "Remember? The earthquake interrupted the group shot we'd planned to take that day at the ice rink."

Scarlet's lips lifted into a sad smile and she rubbed her palm over her flattened stomach. "We're not all together."

I swallowed hard, and the truth tasted bitter. I tore my eyes away, breaking our shared gaze and picked up my phone to look at the photo. Even though we all smiled, a combination of sadness and hope complicated our expressions.

Kai hugged Carlo, and Scarlet and Wendy did the same. Once the last goodbyes were said, Kai gathered the kids and headed out of Pioneer Park.

"So Scarlet gets eaten and what happens to me?"

"You will cross over," I told him, pointing to the rift. "Lure the wolf to the rift with this." I pinched the fabric of Scarlet's cloak. It was soft, silky and nearly invisible like the illusion of the rift itself. I wouldn't miss the strange hood. I wouldn't miss being The Keeper of Stories at all. "Then you'll throw the hood through the rift for Scarlet to put on. The wolf will go for it. I have no doubt he is blinded by his blood thirst for Red."

Scarlet spoke up. "Then Mari presses publish and I let the wolf devour me."

Carlo frowned and looked at his feet. The movement was jerky and awkward but hopefully all traces of his time as Pinocchio would vanish once he took on the role of a new character. I'd written him as a childhood friend of the Cloak Girl. In short, they'd grow up, fall in love, and that was when the Cloak Girl found out that her lifelong friend was really a little prince. They'd grow into a king and a queen and yes, they might lose their daughter—for a day—but I wrote about the victory Mother Gothel had wanted. She was the witch they'd hire to use magic to track Rapunzel and return her from the garden where the toddler-aged child had wandered to munch on some Rampion. It wouldn't even sacrifice *Rapunzel*'s original theme of love and jealousy because I was sure to weave a touch of both within the tale.

"Are we sure this will work?" Carlo asked.

"One hundred percent," Scarlet answered before I could say anything.

I'd wanted to say ninety-nine percent because we'd never done this before. Sure, I remembered my past lives, and I remembered writing *Little Red Riding Hood*. I even remembered being The Poet, The Playwright, The Narrator, and The Author, but I'd never been The Reporter before. This was a first.

When I stayed silent for too long, Carlo cleared his throat and Scarlet glanced at me. I licked my lips and nodded. "One hundred percent," I said as I exchanged a smile with Scarlet.

If she believed, I believed.

I drew in a sharp breath and stooped to grab my laptop from the bench. Each of us found our places. Carlo crossed over into Storyland after Scarlet stripped the hood from her shoulders and stood just outside the rift.

After some waiting, the wolf took the bait. As soon as he dove through the rift, all matted fur and bared fangs, I clicked the button that would officially publish the reporter's post. When "The Curious Case of the Wildlife in Pioneer Park" went live as a report online, the rift disappeared.

The wolf snarled and snagged at the bottom of the hood as Scarlet tried to tug it over her shoulders. Frantically, she yanked the strings and

struggled to tie them around her neck.

Breath left my lungs, and I shoved the laptop aside to stand and run to my best friend. If she couldn't wear the hood, she'd be ripped to shreds rather than swallowed alive. My feet pounded the pavement, heels slamming so hard I'd have bruises later.

"Mari, stop!" She screamed over the wolf's growl.

I froze only a few feet away, and as the wolf's gaze shifted to me, a curse slipped out of my mouth. If he ate me instead, I wouldn't survive. Even if I did, I'd be trapped forever in Storyland, separated from my family while Scarlet was separated from hers.

The moment of distraction gave Scarlet a chance to drape the infamous garment over her body and pull the hood on her head. We locked eyes over the wolf's haunches and she gave me a quick nod before mouthing *thank you*. I would have cried if I had any tears left because this was truly the end. This was the last moment I'd ever speak with Scarlet.

"What big teeth you have," she said as a lure to the wolf.

His tongue snaked out over his teeth. "Better to eat you with." As he turned, his mouth expanded as if unhinged, and I saw a castle in the distance past a field of daisies deep inside of him. Scarlet dropped to a crouch as he snapped his jaws shut around her and then swallowed.

I felt for the gun in my holster and then tilted my head to pop the tension from my neck so I could focus my aim. I raised the weapon and fired round after round after round straight at his skull until the wolf collapsed on the concrete, all blood and fur and claws.

My heart skipped a beat until he finally faded and I was left in the park alone.

I couldn't move, couldn't bring myself to turn around and send the rewritten, fully edited, and final version of "The Curious Case of the Wildlife in Pioneer Park" where Bay Side Media would officially publish it on their main website.

After an indeterminate amount of time, I found my voice again and whispered a phrase Scarlet had said to me long ago. My breath swirled in the darkness like the ghost of a memory.

"It's the death of a fairy tale."

BACK AT HOME, Kai had a feast of takeout food for me to choose from. Unfortunately, I didn't have an appetite for anything, not even my favorite flavor of cheesecake or the perfect crisp of a cream cheese wonton. Basically, I'd never turned down a dish with the word 'cheese' in it before. Another 'first'.

The condo was cozy as a fake fire crackled from the TV screen and Kai sat on the couch, patting for me to take a seat next to him on my favorite cushion. The lights were low and a line of candles flickered from the center of the coffee table.

"I know you like to relax after publishing a tough article," he said. He wasn't wrong. All I normally wanted after a tricky or frightening investigation was to curl up beside him and binge-eat junk food while we watched episodes of a show we'd seen too many times.

I kicked my shoes off and dropped my laptop bag on the floor by the door. Before abandoning it, I stooped to dig out my phone and then crossed the living room to the couch. I accepted Kai's offer but refused to relax until I double-checked one more piece of news. I shot a text to a friend and coworker who was the gossip columnist at Bay Side Media. Elsie responded almost immediately with an answer that the woman who claimed to be the Queen of the Faeries had gone missing only an hour ago. The gossip writer had been tracking her for all the juicy stories until Titania "vanished into thin air".

She went on in the text message to explain that she would use that same language in the post she planned to publish tomorrow. *And I'm not even exaggerating. Titania literally disappeared!*

I managed a half-smile at Elsie's excitement when the phone buzzed again. Another three messages from Elsie popped up on the screen, partially covering my new background photo of our found family in front of the playground.

Oh, and by the way, I made sure Flynn stayed late to publish your article on the main website. It's going live online now.

All at once, my muscles seemed to melt as a weight lifted from my shoulders. For the first time in almost a decade, my mind was completely clear and my body was entirely relaxed despite the gentle throb in my hand and the dull ache in the shoulder that never entirely healed. I hurt, but I felt new, different, fully and wholly mortal... perhaps. Only then did I finally allow myself to sink into the soft cushion and into my husband's warm arms. I nestled my head just below his shoulder and collarbone and blew out a long breath. "Jack went to bed okay?"

"No more endless hours of crying," Kai said. "He didn't fuss at all."

"His magic?"

"Gone."

"What about your magic?" he asked.

"Gone," I said. *One hundred percent gone.*

He brushed away the hair that had escaped from my messy ponytail and tucked it behind my ear. "So you're not Doctor Who anymore?"

I shook my head. "Nope. I'm not The Reporter, just *a* reporter and I honestly can't wait to get back to my normal job. No more fairy tales, no more hunting, no more magic. I'm a reporter, a wife, and a mother and absolutely not a god."

Kai hummed. "Mmm, I beg to differ."

I twisted my neck just to shoot him an annoyed look. "Excuse me?"

"You're a goddess in the bedroom."

I rolled my eyes and reached with my feet for the TV remote on the coffee table. "So, want to binge *Buffy*? This nerdy guy once told me that Buffy is cooler than Doctor Who."

"Sure, oh, except Wendy requested you read the story she wrote before you do anything else." He wiggled out from under me, leaned forward, and plucked a pink spiral notebook from the coffee table. "She said to warn you it was boring without a bad guy so she added a bad guy, but that it's okay because it ends with a happily ever after like a fairy tale should."

I laughed and returned the notebook back to its original spot on the coffee table. "I'll read it later. I'm too busy living my *happily ever after* to read one."

"Good call, *goddess*."

I socked him in the arm and made him swear on the history channel never to call me by that name again. He crossed his heart and then cupped my face in his hand, drawing me closer to him. All thoughts of dying, fairy tales, and our midsummer night in Oz washed away as we melted into a kiss that lasted for an indeterminate amount of time.

Epilogue

Bay Side Media
Author: Mari Rowan
Excerpt from title: The Curious Case of Wildlife in Pioneer Park

Readers, please always be vigilant and be aware of your surroundings.
The world is safer than it once was, but it will never be perfect.
And never, ever go into the woods alone.

UP NEXT: DIVE INTO ANOTHER MAGICAL MURDER INVESTIGATION SERIES WITH NOEMA WOLF FROM THE BEWITCHER'S BEACH PARANORMAL COZY MYSTERIES. THIS IS A SERIES ABOUT ENCHANTING PEOPLE DEALING WITH SMALL-TOWN DRAMA AND FINDING FAMILY THROUGH IT ALL. TAKE A BLAST INTO THE PARANORMAL PAST AND ENJOY THE 1990S NOSTALGIA, THE QUIRKY SUPERNATURAL PEOPLE, AND THE REPRESENTATION OF A MAIN CHARACTER AS MOM. *CAN NOEMA SNIFF OUT THE SUSPECTS BEFORE A MURDEROUS CURSE PUTS HER VIDEO SHOP OUT OF BUSINESS?*

Emily Fluke

PLEASE CONSIDER LEAVING A REVIEW AT YOUR FAVORITE PLACE TO PURCHASE BOOKS IF YOU ENJOYED THIS STORY! ALSO, A SHARE WITH YOUR FRIENDS WOULD BE GREATLY APPRECIATED. MY QUEST AS AN AUTHOR IS TO MAKE OTHERS FEEL SEEN THROUGH THE ADVENTURE OF FICTION. PLEASE REACH OUT TO ME AND LET ME KNOW IF MY STORIES HAVE TOUCHED YOU. YOU, DEAR READER, ARE WHO THIS BOOK WAS WRITTEN FOR.

About the Author

Congenital Heart Defect survivor, Emily Fluke, finds joy and peace through the expression of writing. She is a firm believer that all stories need a little magic and a lot of excitement. Emily and her husband spend their free time wrangling two children and playing video games in their busy California lifestyle. Otherwise, you'll find Emily solving an escape room, running, or writing Magic the Gathering-based poetry.

To stay up to date on new releases and connect with me, visit my website at Emilyfluke.com or follow me on social media under Author Emily Fluke, or @emilyflukefairytales

www.ingramcontent.com/pod-product-compliance
Lightning Source LLC
Chambersburg PA
CBHW020638250626
47154CB00008B/2724